PIZZASAURUS
REX

PIZZASAURUS REX

Written and illustrated by
JUSTIN WAGNER

Colored by
WARREN WUCINICH

Lettered by
MELANIE UJIMORI

Color flats by
JEY ODIN and **DEB GROVES**

Edited by
ROBIN HERRERA

Designed by
KEITH WOOD

AN ONI PRESS PUBLICATION

Published by **Oni Press, Inc.**

JOE NOZEMACK founder & chief financial officer
JAMES LUCAS JONES publisher
CHARLIE CHU v.p. of creative & business development
BRAD ROOKS director of operations
MELISSA MESZAROS director of publicity
MARGOT WOOD director of sales
RACHEL REED marketing manager
TROY LOOK director of design & production
HILARY THOMPSON senior graphic designer
KATE Z. STONE junior graphic designer
SONJA SYNAK junior graphic designer
ANGIE KNOWLES digital prepress lead
ARI YARWOOD executive editor
ROBIN HERRERA senior editor
DESIREE WILSON associate editor
ALISSA SALLAH administrative assistant
JUNG LEE logistics associate

onipress.com
facebook.com/onipress
twitter.com/onipress
onipress.tumblr.com
instagram.com/onipress

First Edition: July 2018

ISBN 978-1-62010-507-8
eISBN 978-1-62010-508-5

Pizzasaurus Rex, July 2018. Published by Oni Press, Inc. 1319 SE Martin Luther King Jr. Blvd., Suite 240, Portland, OR 97214.

Library of Congress Control Number: 2017960736

10 9 8 7 6 5 4 3 2 1

Printed in China.

CHAPTER 1

SCIENCE FAIR!
GASP!
IT'S AS IF ALL MY WILDEST DREAMS HAVE COME TRUE.
TIME TO SHINE...
HEY DOODOOMAN, NICE SCIENCE PROJECT.
WHUZZAT?!

ACTUALLY, THE NAME'S ***DUDERMAN***, BUT THANKS! IT DOES LOOK NICE, DOESN'T IT?
BY NICE I MEANT DOODOO... SAME AS YOUR DUMB NAME.
SHOULDA ENTERED IT IN THE SUCK FAIR INSTEAD.
WAIT, THAT'S A THING?
YEAH, IT'S A THING... A THING I JUST MADE UP.
NICE!
GASP! YOU'RE A LIAR!
WAIT, AM I BEING BULLIED?
YES, YOU ARE. NOW SHOW US YOUR DUMB PROJECT BEFORE I SMASH YOUR FACE.
OKAY! IT'S A ***PIZZA-CANO!***
BY MY CALCULATIONS, IF YOU SIMPLY ADD CRUSHED TOMATOES, OREGANO, AND A BLEND OF ARTISANAL CHEESES, YOU CAN TURN YOUR AVERAGE VOLCANO INTO A PIZZA FACTORY!
PIZZA-CANO
ENDING WORLD HUNGER!
I HATE IT.

WHO HATES PIZZA?
I DO!
I HATE PIZZA!
YOU DO KNOW THEY MAKE GLUTEN-FREE?
I HAVE A GLUTEN ALLERGY!
I HATE GLUTEN-FREE PIZZA!
IT TASTES LIKE GARBAGE!
IT MAKES ME SO MAD I WANNA DESTROY A SCIENCE FAIR PROJECT!
YOU COULD DESTROY LAURA'S... SAVE HER A TRIP TO THE TRASH CAN.
SOLAR SYSTE
HEY!
SORRY, LAURA BUT C'MON... A SOLAR SYSTEM?
AMATEUR HOUR OVER HERE, AMIRITE?
RRRGH!
AAAGHHHH!
CRIPES!

CANO
STOP! YOUR GLUTEN ALLERGY HAS BLINDED YOU WITH RAGE!
AND I WISH THERE WAS SOMETHING I COULD DO ABOUT IT, BUT I'M CRIPPLED WITH FEAR!
AND THAT'S THAT.
I JUST-- I CAN'T-- SIGH.
MY FELLOW BULLIES, I GROW WEARY OF DOODOOMAN'S SUCKINESS.
PLEASE DISPATCH OF THIS LOSER, LEST I LOSE MY LUNCH.
I DON'T SUCK! SOMEDAY I'LL DO SOMETHING TOTALLY RADICAL!
AND YOU'LL ALL BE LIKE, "MAN, THAT DUDE IS...IS...RAD!"
NOT LIKELY... ONCE A LOSER, ALWAYS A LOSER.
OOOF!
THIS IS ONE OF THOSE MOMENTS I'M BOUND TO REPEAT UNTIL I FIND THE VALUABLE LIFE LESSON IN IT.
QUIT TALKING TO YOURSELF, CREEPY FREAK!

SOMEDAY...20 YEARS LATER
DUDERMANLABS
DR. JEREMY DUDERMAN
HEAD OF RADICALITY STUDIES
AND YEAH, THAT'S A THING
GASP!
THAT SOMEDAY I WAS JUST TALKING ABOUT 20 YEARS AGO HAS COME.
TIME TO SHINE...
YOU SHINE, JEREMY DUDERMAN. YOU SHINE SO BRIGHT--
AHEM...DUDE, ARE YOU CRYING?
WHAAAAAT?! NO WAY!
BUT EVEN IF I WAS, THAT'D BE ALRIGHT, RIGHT? KIND OF A BIG DAY FOR ME.
NO, IT WOULD NOT BE OKAY. AND STOP TALKING TO YOURSELF, WEIRDO.
WAIT, AM I BEING BULLIED AGAIN?
DR. DUDERMAN, ARE YOU--

I WASN'T CRYING!
--READY TO START THE PRESENTATION, IS WHAT I WAS GOING TO SAY!
JEEPERS, I'M SORRY, LIZZIE. A LITTLE EDGY RIGHT NOW.
TOTALLY FINE. IT'S A BIG DAY FOR YOU. ALSO, IT'S LEXI--
YES. AND I THANK YOU FOR ALL YOUR ASSISTANCE, LINDSAY.
WHY THE FUDGE IS THIS NOT WORKING?
SMASH!
SQORK! WHAT DID I SAY ABOUT FARTING AROUND IN MY WIRING?!
GEE, SQORK IS SORRY. SQORK WAS BORED.
BUT I GUESS NOW YOU COULD SAY SQORK IS WIRED! RIGHT?!
SIGH. C'MON, SQORK. BACK TO YOUR ENCLOSURE.
WHAT THE HECK IS THAT THING?

OH, IGNORE HIM. JUST A **FAILED** EXPERIMENT IN FELINE GENETIC MANIPULATION.
SHOULDA ENTERED HIM IN THE SUCK FAIR!
NICE!
WAIT, THAT'S A TH--
REALLY? WE'RE DOING THIS **AGAIN?**
ACTUALLY, NO, WE'RE NOT-- JUST SHOW US YOUR DUMB PRESENTATION.
MY ABILITY TO FEIGN INTEREST IS WANING.
OKAY!
AS YOU ALL KNOW, I'VE SPENT YEARS TRYING TO DEFINE THE ESSENCE OF RADICALITY, AND HAVE FOUND IT TO BE A MOST ELUSIVE FORCE...
A FORCE WHOSE ORIGIN IS ALIEN TO THIS DIMENSION...
WELL, GENTLEMEN, I HAVE INVENTED A MACHINE THAT MAY JUST ALLOW ONE A MERE GLIMPSE INTO THE ABYSS OF **RADICALITY.**
I PRESENT TO YOU...

THE REALITY ALTERNATIVE DIMENSIONATOR!
OR R.A.D. FOR SHORT!
RAD
YOU'RE AN IDIOT.
ALSO, I'M LEAVING.
RAD
JUST WAIT TIL I TURN IT ON! WHICH I ALREADY DID, ACCIDENTALLY!
YOU WHAT?!
THIS REMOTE WAS IN MY BACK POCKET...
MUSTA BUTT-DIALED...
YOU GUYS SMELL SMOKE?
YES! BECAUSE YOUR DUMB IDIOT MACHINE IS SMOKING, YOU DUMB IDIOT!
CRIPES!
OUTTATHEWAY!
MOVE IT!
DR. DUDERMAN!
JEREMY!

GASP!
SPLUT!
RAD
RAD

SOMEONE ORDER A ***RADICAL REPTILE*** FROM ***ANOTHER DIMENSION?!***
ACK! ACK!
AT A LOSS FOR WORDS, DUDE? I GET IT...
...I'D FREAK IF I MET ME, TOO!

NICE TO MEET YA ANYWAY, BRO.
GASP!
WHUZZAT?!
THERE HE IS! OPEN FIRE!
YOU DON'T HAVE TO YELL, I'M STANDING RIGHT NEXT TO YOU.
WAIT, WHERE'S MY GUN?
LAY OFF! YOU KNOW HE YELLS WHEN HE GETS EXCITED!
OOF!
KEEP FIRING! THEY'RE BEHIND THAT TABLE!
I HAVE EYES, STUPID.
HEY! HE HAS FEELINGS, Y'KNOW.
NO HE DOESN'T! WE'RE ROBOTS! AND WHY AREN'T THESE LASERS BLOWING UP THAT DUMB TABLE TO BITS?!
HMM, MUST BE MADE OF WOOD. THESE THINGS DON'T SHOOT THROUGH THAT STUFF.
HONESTLY, I DON'T KNOW WHAT THEY SHOOT THROUGH. THEY MOSTLY JUST BOUNCE AROUND.
UGH! WHAT KIND OF IDIOT INVENTED THESE?!

YOU WATCH YOUR TONGUE, SOLDIER!
THAT WEAPON YOU HOLD WAS CREATED BY NONE OTHER THAN OUR FATHER, THE GREAT EMPEROR BUZZKILL!
BUZZKILL, SHMUZZKILL... WHAT'S HE DONE FOR ME LATELY?
GASP!
RAD
THAT'S RIGHT, I SAID IT!
HE MAY HAVE CREATED ME, BUT I HAVE MY OWN FEELINGS!
MY OWN DREAMS!
AS A MATTER OF FACT, I AM NO LONGER POSER DRONE 37...
I CHOOSE MY OWN NAME...
37
...FROM THIS DAY FORWARD, I WILL BE KNOWN AS NATHAN!
BOOM!
YEAHHH, EMOTIONAL INHIBITOR DEVICE...
ANYONE ELSE FEELING FREE WILL-Y?
NOPE. BUT I HAVE THE STRANGEST FEELING--
HE SAID THE F-WORD!
EVERYONE STOP HAVING FEELINGS!
UGH, POSERS...
BOOM!

IT'S AS IF ALL MY WILDEST DREAMS HAVE COME TRUE...
YES. I AM AWESOME. I GET IT A LOT.
UNGHHH... WHAT'S GOING ON?
HOLY MOTHER OF BABES!
I FEEL SO STRANGE...
SO...
...RADICAL.
AGH!
THE RADICALITY! IT'S SPREADING! SHOOT HER!
LIKE DESTROYING A BEAUTIFUL FLOWER...
SHUT UP!

RAD
WHY AM I THE ONLY ONE WHO'S NOT RADICAL?
NOT THE ONLY ONE!
HERE SQORK IS! SAME OL' SQORK!
SIGH.
CAN SOMEONE EXPLAIN WHAT'S GOING ON?! WHO ARE YOU?!
THE NAME'S REX... REX RADITUDE.
THE PIZZASAURUS!
SOOOOO RAD.
YEAH, WELL, YOU'RE SUPPOSED TO BE SHOOTING HIM!
OH, RIGHT.

SICK OLLIE.
LOOK AWAY!
INDY NOSEBONE.
DON'T LOOK DIRECTLY AT THE RADICALITY!
INTO A MANUAL?! WHAT?!
NOOOO!

SQORK.
THIS IS LITERALLY THE BEST DAY OF MY LIFE.
I STILL DON'T GET WHAT'S GOING ON.
OH YEAH? GET THIS!
I WAS TALKING TO THE GIRL, STUPID!
GET WHAT?
WELL, EXCUUUUUSE ME FOR LIVING... RUDE MUCH?
SAY GOODBYE TO YOUR FACE, DINOSAUR...CUZ IT'S ABOUT TO BE BLASTED OFF!
NOT IF HIS FACE IS MADE OF WOOD, THOUGH.
FACES ARE MADE OF WOOD?
41

NO! NOT THE PIZZA-TAR!
THAT'S RIGHT! AND GUITAR WAILING 101 IS NOW IN SESSION!
OOOH! GUITAR LESSONS!
COVER YOUR EARS!
CAN'T... HE'S ALREADY GOT ME.
DITTO.
HEH HEH, TALK ABOUT A FACE-MELTER, RIGHT?
WE'RE GONNA DIE AND YOU'RE MAKING JOKES?!
MAYBE HUMOR IS THE ONLY WAY I CAN DEAL WITH IT!
FAIR ENOUGH.

YES!

CLASS DISMISSED.
WOOOOO!
WHOA, FORGOT YOU DUDES WERE BACK THERE...
WHAT SAY WE GET SOME GRUB, MY NEW BROS AND BRO-ETTE?
UM, FIRST CAN YOU EXPLAIN WHAT JUST HAPP--
SURE! WHAT'S YOUR FAVORITE FOOD?!
DUH.
LET US DINE, MY DUDES!
YAY!
RAD
I FEEL LIKE I'M FORGETTING TO TURN SOMETHING OFF...
EH, WHATEVER.
RAD

THE RAD ONE.
HE HAS BEEN HERE.
GAH!

THERE'S PIZZA EVERYWHERE, BOSS. I'M BETTING YOU-KNOW-WHO WAS HERE.
REALLY?! DID THE PILE OF YOUR DISMEMBERED AND/OR MELTED COMRADES NOT TIP YOU OFF?!
NATHAN!
NOOOO!
UGH, PIZZA! I HATE PIZZA!
HOW DARE THAT WRETCHED REPTILE SPREAD HIS DISGUSTING FILTH TO ANOTHER DIMENSION THAT IS PROBABLY RIGHTFULLY OURS?!
YES, EMPEROR BUZZKILL! WE WILL DISPOSE OF THE RAD ONE'S EXCREMENT AND THEN WE WILL DISPOSE OF HIM.
WHO HATES PIZZA?
RIGHT?

I DO! I HAVE A GLUTEN ALLERGY!
YOU KNOW THEY MAKE--
PLEASE SAY GLUTEN-FREE SO I CAN DESTROY YOU!
JEEZ LOUISE, STRESSED MUCH?
CALM YOURSELF, MY MASTER. THE PIZZASAURUS WILL BE DESTROYED AND SUCKINESS WILL BE RESTORED TO THE UNIVERSE.
LEAVE IT TO ME, YOUR HUMBLE SERVANT, SERGEANT SURGE.
ALL HAIL EMPEROR BUZZKILL!
FOR YOUR SAKE, I HOPE YOU HAVE A DETAILED PLAN... I GROW WEARY OF FALSE PROMISES.
UHH...
DUHHHH, WE HAVE A PLAN, BOSS!

NO DINOSAUR CAN DUH-FEAT...
THE *E-RAD-ICATOR!*
AND DAS WASSUP...
ERADICATOR
HOW THE HECK DID YOU MORONS EVEN FIT THAT THING THROUGH THE PORTAL THINGY?!
YOU IDIOTS!!!
HOW ARE WE SUPPOSED TO RETURN TO OUR DIMENSION NOW?!
WELL, DR. DUMBDUMB LEFT THE BLUEPRINTS...
GIVE US, LIKE, A WEEK?
HEH HEH, LOOKS LIKE WE'RE LOCKED IN ON FINALLY DESTROYING THAT PIZZASAURUS...
AMIRITE?

CHAPTER
2

YOU GOT THIS, JEREMY...
PINEY PINES MALL
PINEY PINES
TODAY: YET ANOTHER SCIENCE FAIR
JUST A LITTLE SCIENCE FAIR...
A SCIENCE FAIR NOT UNLIKE THE ONE YOU WERE HUMILIATED AT ALL THOSE YEARS AGO.
WICKED XTREME SCIENCE FAIR!
WHOLE PIPE
PIZZA
S-D SHADES
JUST A LITTLE HUMILIATION THAT GREW TO DEFINE YOUR EXISTENCE THE PAST TWO DECADES.
ALSO, KINDA LIKE THE HUMILIATION FROM, LIKE, YESTERDAY...
YO, CHECK THE SCIENCE DUDE TALKING TO HIMSELF.
I KNOW, WHAT A CREEP.
WOW, EVEN MY OWN MIND IS CREEPED OUT BY ME.
NOT YOUR MIND, BRO. TURN AROUND MUCH?

WHUZZAT?!
YEAH, DUDE, YOU'RE ON.
OH, RIGHT. I'M IN THE MIDDLE OF A PRESENTATION. HEH HEH.
WHOA, WICKED TRAPPER KEEPER.
RIGHT?! IT'S AN ***X-TREME-O*** THREE-RING BINDER, TRICKED OUT WITH ALL OF MY ILLEST SCIENTIFIC FINDINGS!
I'VE HAD IT FOR, LIKE, EVER!
DON'T NEED YOUR LIFE STORY... JUST TAKE THE COMPLIMENT.
ALSO, WHERE'S MY FREE PIZZA, DUDE?
UMMM, I DON'T KNOW WHO TOLD YOU THERE'D BE FREE PIZZA, BUT THEY WERE MISTAKEN.
NOW, ON WITH THE--
LOOK, BRO, I LIKE TWO THINGS IN THIS LIFE: FREE STUFF AND PIZZA. BOTH OF WHICH WERE PROMISED TO ME.
TRUE.

LOOK, I THINK I'D REMEMBER IF I WAS LIKE, "HEY GUYS, FREE PIZZA!"
WHAAAT?!
FREE PIZZA?!
UH OH...
YEAH!
UNGA!
DUDE, DID YOU HEAR?! THIS NERD IS GIVIN' OUT FREE PIZZA!
EH, PIZZA IS ALRIGHT.
ARE YOU KIDDING ME?!
OF COURSE I AM! RUSH THE STAGE!
WOOWOO!
OKAY, SO I DON'T REALLY HAVE PIZZA WITH ME RIGHT NOW!
MAYBE WE CAN GET SOME KIND OF VOUCHER SITUATION HAPPENING!
OH, I GOT YOUR FREE PIZZA...

RIGHT HERE!!!
YEAHHH!!!
FREE BASKETBALL PIZZA!
BUNG
I-I-I CAN'T SEE ANYTHING.
DUDE! THAT DINOSAUR DUNKED YOUR FACE OFF!
THERE'S A DINOSAUR?

SORRY, DOC, LOOKED LIKE YOUR SCIENCE THINGY NEEDED A BOOST.
AND BY BOOST, I MEAN SLAM DUNKING THIS UNRULY CROWD'S FACES OFF.
YEAH, THANKS. I WAS KINDA DYING OUT THERE.
AND THAT'S WHAT MAKES US A GREAT TEAM, MAN...
YOU SET IT UP, AND I SLAMMA-JAMMA IT SO HARD, IT EXPLODES PIZZA SLICES ALL OVER PEOPLE'S FACES.
WE--WE'RE A TEAM?
OF COURSE, BROSEPH.
NOW, ARE YOU MANIACS READY TO LISTEN TO MY MAN JAM ON SOME SCIENCE?!
YES.
HERE, LEMME HELP.
JUST A SEC-- THIS BINDER HAS SEEN BETTER DAYS.

WOOOOO!!
YOU DON'T HAVE TO DO TH--
YOU LOOK DIFFERENT... NEW LAB COAT?
OH, THIS? I WOULDN'T NORMALLY WEAR SOMETHING SO BOLD--
BUT LATELY, I DUNNO, IT'S LIKE I'M BRIMMING WITH CONFIDENCE.
I JUST WANTED TO LOOK MY BEST F--
THAT'S AWESOME! I'M SO HAPPY FOR YOU!
I'M SORRY! I YELL WHEN I'M CLEARLY JEALOUS OF SOMEONE ELSE'S RADICAL LIFE TRANS-FORMATION!
THANK YOU!

HERE, WATCH THIS STUPID VIDEO I MADE.
PLAY
SIGH.
WELCOME TO THE AGE OF ***RADICALITY,*** MY FRIENDS...
MY MAIN MAN HERE, DR. JEREMY DUDERMAN, CREATED THE ***R.A.D.*** MACHINE...
EXHIBIT A
A THING THAT, LIKE, PORTALIZES SPACE AND TIME...
EXHIBIT A
ALLOWING YOURS TRULY TO COME IN AND SUBSEQUENTLY ROCK THIS WORLD.
BEHOLD, MY HOME, ***THE PIZZARELLAVERSE!*** A DIMENSION WHERE RADICALITY ABOUNDS.
BUT THERE ARE SOME SERIOUS BUTTHEADS WHOSE SOLE PURPOSE IS TO E-***RAD***-ICATE ALL RADICALITY FROM EXISTENCE...
THUS SHIFTING THE BALANCE OF THE UNIVERSE FROM RAD TO SUCK.
BUT DON'T WORRY YOUR LITTLE NOGGINS ABOUT THAT. I GOT THIS LOCKED.
AND THE RESULT OF MY AWESOME PRESENCE IN THIS DIMENSION?
RAD-IATION IS SWEEPING THE NATION!
SEEMS LIKE THE DOC'S INVENTION HAS THE DORKIEST DORK BECOMING THE DUDIEST DUDE!

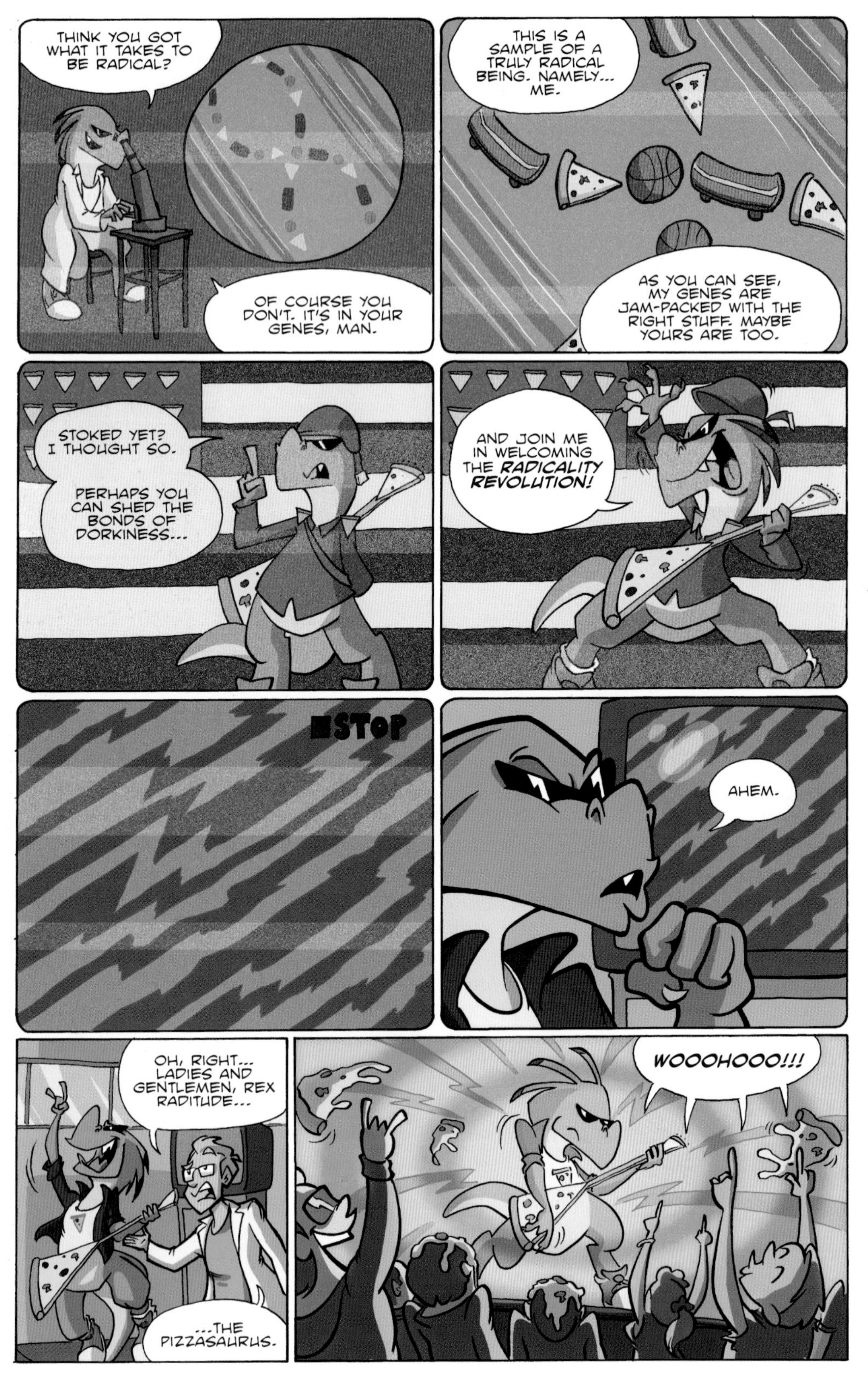
THINK YOU GOT WHAT IT TAKES TO BE RADICAL?
OF COURSE YOU DON'T. IT'S IN YOUR GENES, MAN.
THIS IS A SAMPLE OF A TRULY RADICAL BEING. NAMELY... ME.
AS YOU CAN SEE, MY GENES ARE JAM-PACKED WITH THE RIGHT STUFF. MAYBE YOURS ARE TOO.
STOKED YET? I THOUGHT SO.
PERHAPS YOU CAN SHED THE BONDS OF DORKINESS...
AND JOIN ME IN WELCOMING THE *RADICALITY REVOLUTION!*
STOP
AHEM.
OH, RIGHT... LADIES AND GENTLEMEN, REX RADITUDE...
...THE PIZZASAURUS.
WOOOHOOO!!!

I FOUND THAT VIDEO TO BE BOTH EDUCATIONAL AND UTTERLY WICKED.
I AM TRULY GRATEFUL TO HAVE HAD EYEBALLS WITH WHICH TO WATCH IT.
RUB IT IN, WHY DON'T YA?!
HOW ARE YOU EVEN TALKING?
ANY QUESTIONS?
YES, YOU... THE DUDE WITH THE KILLER SHADES.
SCIENCE DUDE WAS EXPOSED TO THE RAD-IATION...
...AND HE'S STILL SUCKIER THAN THE SUCKIEST-WHATEVER-SUCK-THING.
OKAY, FIRST OFF, THAT WASN'T REALLY A QUESTION.
AND SECONDLY, I'LL HAVE YOU KNOW--
IT'S OKAY, REX...
I HAVEN'T RUN FURTHER TESTS, BUT IT'S MY BELIEF THAT PERHAPS RADICALITY IS LATENT IN CERTAIN SUBJECTS...
IT MAY TAKE TIME FOR THE RAD-IATION TO TAKE EFFECT.

OR... NOT.
OR MAYBE I'LL LIVE OUT THE REST OF MY DAYS AS A SHELL OF A MAN...
...A PILE OF WASTED POTENTIAL THAT SLUGS ALONG WHILE EVERYONE ELSE GETS WHAT THEY WANT...
...UNTIL DEATH'S SWEET RELEASE ALLOWS ME RESPITE FROM THE PAIN OF LIVING.
WOW.
YES, WOW... YOU'RE ALL STANDING BEFORE A TRUE GENIUS!
SURELY, YOU MUST HAVE SOME INTELLIGENT QUESTIONS!
YOU'RE HOT.
UGH, STILL NOT EVEN A QUESTION.

HEY HEY! SPEAKING OF DUMB QUESTIONS... WHO WANTS MORE PIZZA?!
I DO!
YEAH!
OVER HERE!
LOOK LORI--
LEXI.
RIGHT. I APPRECIATE YOU KEEPING THIS THING TOGETHER, BUT THEY'RE RIGHT... I DON'T BELONG HERE.
I'M NOT RADICAL...
THAT'S NOT TRUE! LOOK WHAT YOU'VE DONE!
WITHOUT YOU REX WOULDN'T EVEN BE HERE!
AND ME, WELL, YOU'VE--
UGH. IT DOESN'T MATTER! EVERYONE'S GONNA TURN RADICAL AND I'LL BE LEFT BEHIND LIKE A TOTAL LOSER!
SQORK WILL STILL BE YOUR FRIEND!
SIGH. SOMEONE KILL ME NOW.
DUHHHH, YOU ASKED FOR IT!
GASP!

YO! PREPARE YOUR BUTTS FOR SOME SERIOUS POUNDING!
DUH, YEAH, WE'RE HERE TO POUND YOUR BUTTS INTO OBLIVION!
REALLY WEIRD THING TO SAY...
GET BENT
IT'S NOT WEIRD! IT'S COOL! NOW BLAST THIS FOOL!
HEH HEH, RHYMES.

DUH, WELL, SAY GOODBYE TO RADICALITY!
AND HOLA TO *SUCK* CUZ THIS LASER CANNON DOES THAT...
THAT'S WHY WE CALL IT--
JUST SHOOT THE DUDE ALREADY, GEEZ.
NO!
AGGGHHH!
GASP!
STRANGE... I FEEL PERFECTLY NORMAL.
THERE'S A SHOCKER.
TRY SHOOTING SOMEONE WHO'S ACTUALLY RADICAL WITH THAT THING!
SIGH. A NEW LOW...
DUH, YOU ASKED FOR IT!
LITERALLY!

NOOO!
SO I SAYS TO DALE, I SAYS, "I KNOW THIS IS A SELLER'S MARKET, BUT I'M ABOUT TO WALK ON THIS WHOLE DEAL."
I-I-IS THAT A BLUETOOTH?!
RUN FOR YOUR LIVES!
WELL, NOT REALLY LIVES...
YOU KNOW WHAT HE MEANS!
EVERYONE COOL OUT...
I GOT THIS.
HEY, DUDES, WANNA SEE IF THAT THING CAN TAKE OUT ONE BAD DUDE?
DUH, SURE?
RHETORICAL MUCH?
SHOOT HIM?

YO! CRANK THE POWER ON THIS THING!
I CAN'T!
IT'S MAXED OUT!
MEH
BLEH
HUH?
GUH?!
SUCK-O-METER

WHAT IS WITH THESE LASERS?
I'LL TELL YA WHAT'S WITH THEM...
THEY SUCK.
MEH, WAS EXPECTING A BIT MORE FROM YOU CHUMPS.
YO, DON'T POUND OUR BUTTS, PLEASE!
DUH, YEAH, WE LEARNED OUR LESSON!
AU CONTRAIRE, MON FRERE...
I MAY HAVE BROKEN YOUR DUMB RAY GUN, BUT NOW I SHALL BREAK YOUR SPIRIT IN A LITTLE TWO-ON-TWO B-BALL ACTION.
DOC, YOU'VE JUST BEEN DRAFTED TO *TEAM RADITUDE!*
WE ARE SOOOO NOT DOING THIS...

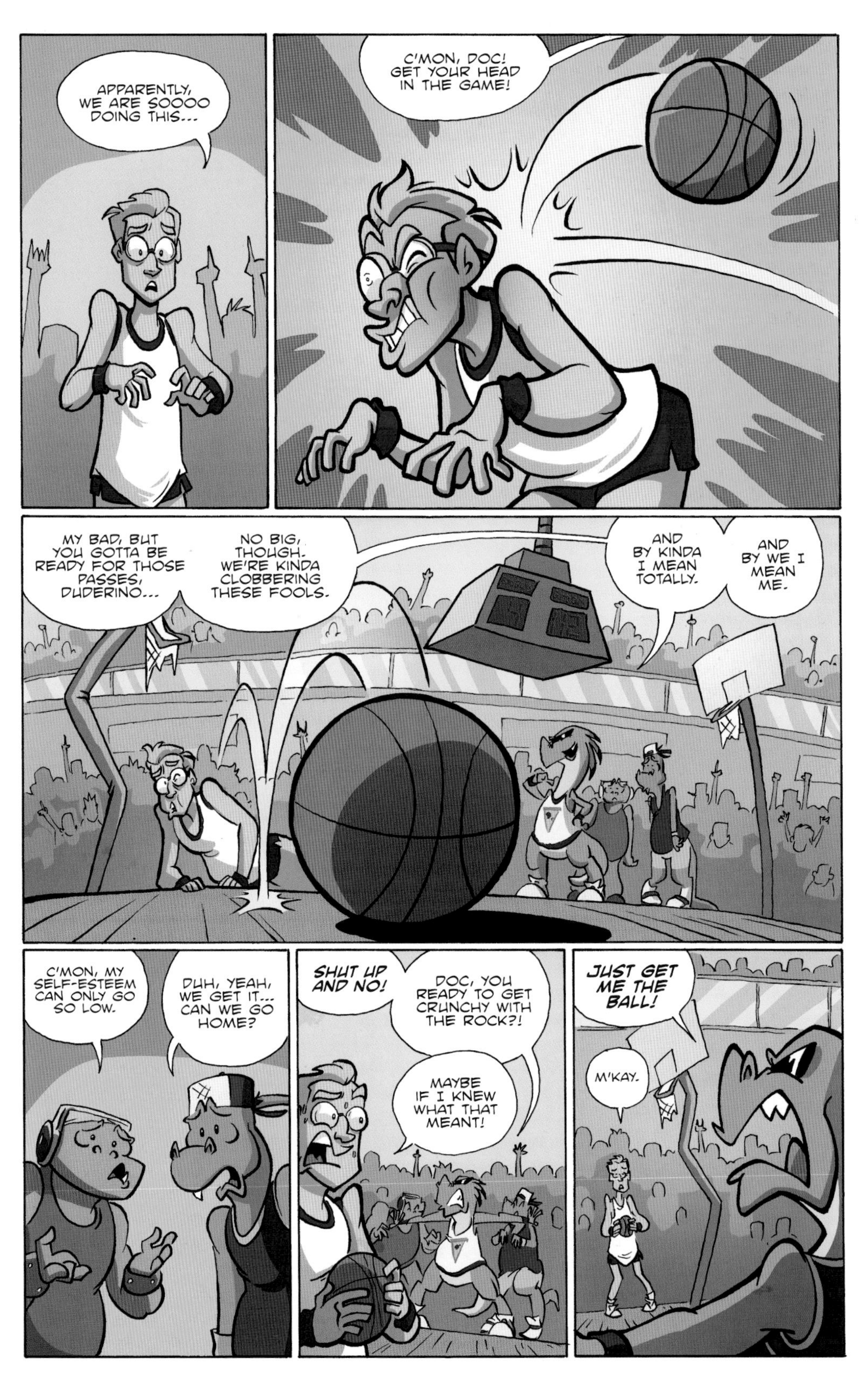

APPARENTLY, WE ARE SOOOO DOING THIS...
C'MON, DOC! GET YOUR HEAD IN THE GAME!
MY BAD, BUT YOU GOTTA BE READY FOR THOSE PASSES, DUDERINO...
NO BIG, THOUGH. WE'RE KINDA CLOBBERING THESE FOOLS.
AND BY KINDA I MEAN TOTALLY.
AND BY WE I MEAN ME.
C'MON, MY SELF-ESTEEM CAN ONLY GO SO LOW.
DUH, YEAH, WE GET IT... CAN WE GO HOME?
SHUT UP AND NO!
DOC, YOU READY TO GET CRUNCHY WITH THE ROCK?!
MAYBE IF I KNEW WHAT THAT MEANT!
JUST GET ME THE BALL!
M'KAY.

YO! COVER HIM!
DUH, WE SHOULD BOTH COVER HIM...
CUZ THAT OTHER DUDE SUUUUCKS!
SHUT UP! I'M TRYING MY BEST!
PASS IT TO ME, DOC!
HEY, MAN, YOUR SHOES ARE UNTIED.
YEAH RIGHT...
NICE TRY, LOSER!
I TRY TO HELP HIM AND HE YELLS AT ME...
HOW RUDE?!
GAH!

NO WAY...
IT MIGHT...
FROM DOWNTOWN...
OR NOT.
IT'S OKAY, DOC... I'LL FINISH THIS!
APPRECIATE THE HUSTLE, THOUGH!
whimper
IT'S GOTTA BE THE SHOES!
SHUT UP!

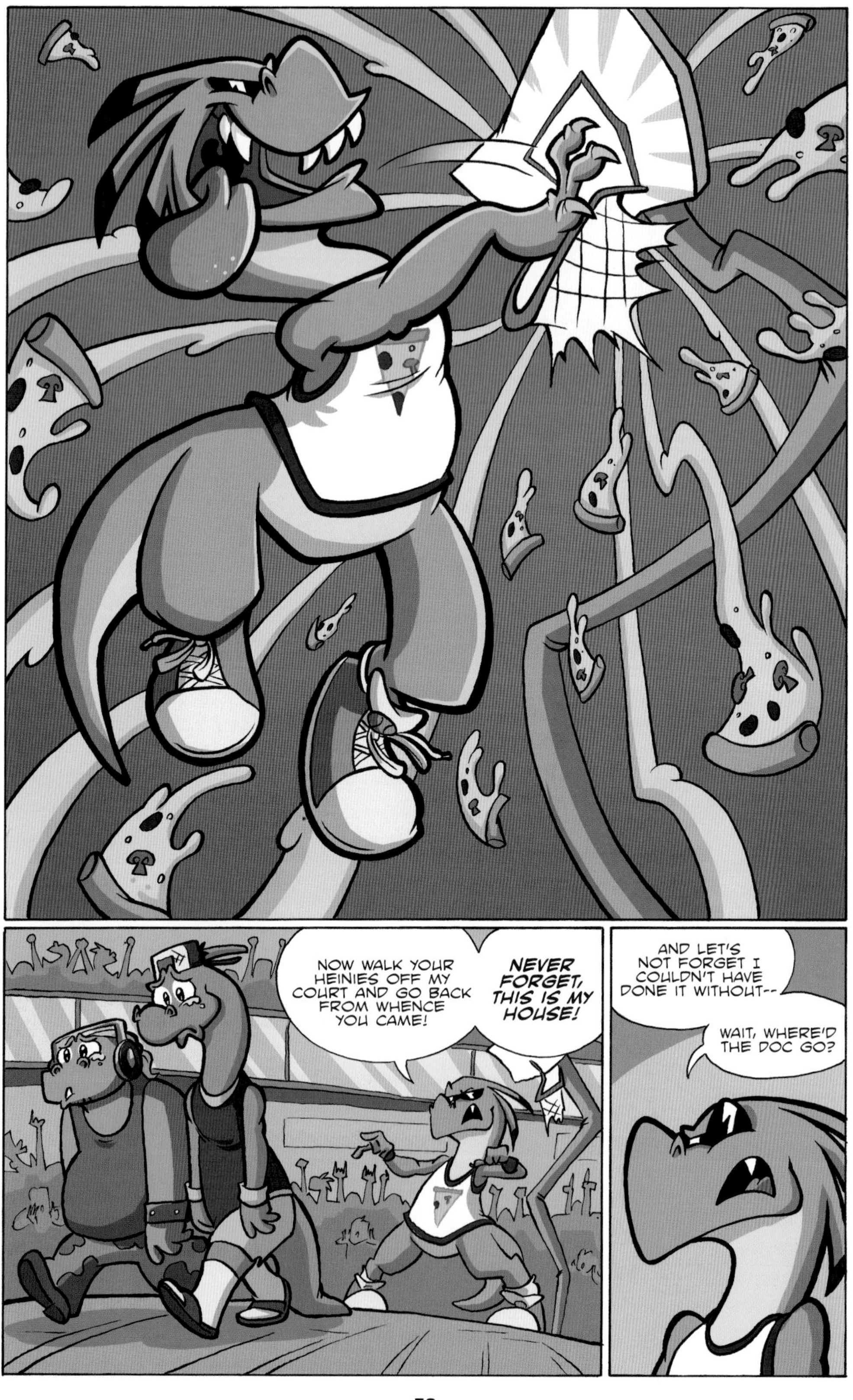
NOW WALK YOUR HEINIES OFF MY COURT AND GO BACK FROM WHENCE YOU CAME!
NEVER FORGET, THIS IS MY HOUSE!
AND LET'S NOT FORGET I COULDN'T HAVE DONE IT WITHOUT--
WAIT, WHERE'D THE DOC GO?

FOOD COURT
SIGH.
THERE YOU ARE! I'VE BEEN LOOKING ALL OVER FOR YOU!
GROAN.
OH, WELL, IF YOU DON'T WANT ME AROUND I CAN--
THAT WAS MY STOMACH GROANING, ACTUALLY...
EATING SIXTEEN CINNA-BUNS ISN'T TURNING OUT TO BE MY BRIGHTEST IDEA.
GROAN.
STOMACH AGAIN?
NOPE. THAT WAS ALL ME. I AM PATHETIC. AND ALSO HAVE NOTHING.
BUT THIS, THIS IS ALL I HAVE NOW. THIS CINNAMON CONFECTION.
AND MUCH LIKE THE CINNA-BUN, I HAD ALL THE POTENTIAL FOR AWESOMENESS, BUT WITH THAT FIRST BITE YOU REALIZE IT'S JUST BRIMMING WITH MEDIOCRITY.
JEEZ.

DON'T BE SILLY...
I'VE SEEN YOU ACCOMPLISH GREAT THINGS...
YOU DON'T NEED TO DUNK, OR SKATEBOARD, OR PLAY GUITAR. JUST BE YOU.
YOU ARE MORE THAN A CINNA-BUN, JEREMY.
I PROMISE YOU THAT.
DON'T BE SAD!
SQORK IS YOUR **NUMBER ONE FAN!**
FANNY FAN
GET IT?! **FAN?!**
UGH. I THINK I'D LIKE TO BE ALONE FOR A BIT.
C'MON, SQORK. LET'S GET YOU SOME ICE CREAM OR SOMETHING.
SCREAM!
GET IT?! SQORK "SCREAMED FOR ICE CREAM"!
SIGH.

SPACEY SPACE STORAGE. CURRENT/TEMPORARY BAD GUY LAIR.
SPACEY SPACE
S.S. STORAGE
UTTER DISAPPOINTMENTS! ALL OF YOU!
IT'S LIKE YOU'RE DELIBERATELY TRYING TO FAIL!
I THINK HE'S TALKING TO YOU...
OH, GET BENT.
YOU GET BENT!
NO ONE IS GETTING BENT!
GO SUCK AN EGG!
YOU GO SUCK AN EGG!
NO ONE IS SUCKING ANY EGGS, EITHER!
WE NEED TO DEVISE A NEW PLAN.
SO EVERYONE RELAX!
SERIOUSLY, SUCK AN EGG.

SHUT UP! SHUT UP! SHUT UP!
FOOLS! I WILL MAKE THE DINOSAUR COME TO ME...
AND I WILL DESTROY HIM.
SOLID PLAN.
AND MAYBE WE SHOULD GET SIDE JOBS CUZ THIS STORAGE SPACE AIN'T GONNA PAY FOR ITSELF.
LET'S NOT AND SAY WE DID.
UGH.
WHAT?! I'M TRYIN' TO GET A CATCH PHRASE GOIN' UP IN THIS PIECE!
WELL, HOW ABOUT TRYING SOMETHING ORIGINAL?
SILENCE!
ENOUGH OF THIS FOOLISH-NESS!
OKAAAY THENNNN...

CHAPTER
3

WHATTUP, PARTY PEOPLE?!
IT'S ME, YOUR HOST, MARK MULDOOD...
...AND WELCOME BACK TO THE **X-TREME-O** ARENA WHERE I'M ACCOMPANIED BY OUR CHAMPION THUS FAR.
REX, YOU'VE ABSOLUTELY STOMPED THE COMPETITION TO GET HERE!
I MEAN, THE ATTEMPTS TO BEAT YOU WERE COMPLETELY FEEBLE AND DOWNRIGHT PATHETIC!
YEAH, WELL, WE'RE JUST KIDS.
NOT AN EXCUSE.
WE TRIED OUR BEST?
SHUT UP?

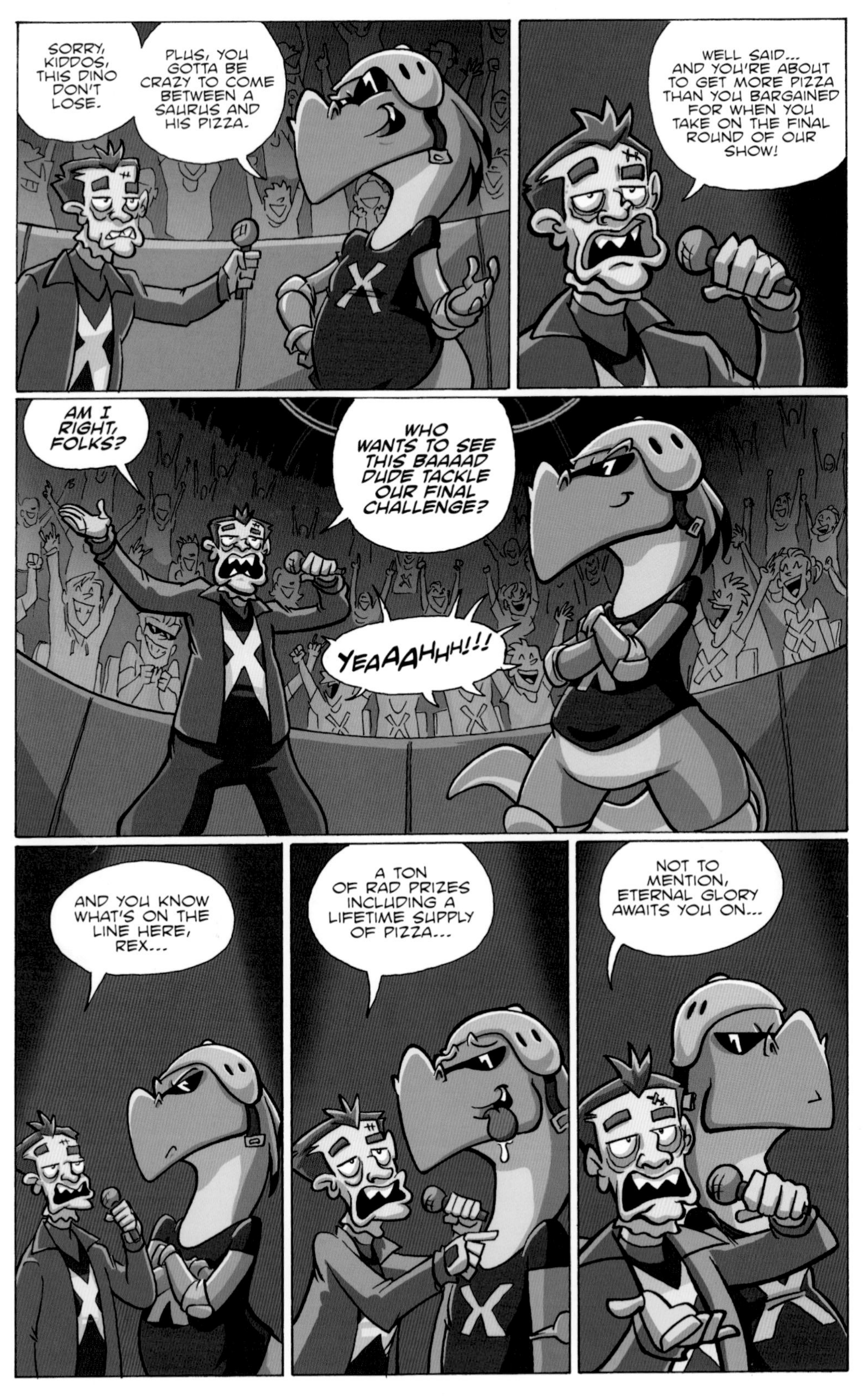
SORRY, KIDDOS, THIS DINO DON'T LOSE.
PLUS, YOU GOTTA BE CRAZY TO COME BETWEEN A SAURUS AND HIS PIZZA.
WELL SAID... AND YOU'RE ABOUT TO GET MORE PIZZA THAN YOU BARGAINED FOR WHEN YOU TAKE ON THE FINAL ROUND OF OUR SHOW!
AM I RIGHT, FOLKS?
WHO WANTS TO SEE THIS BAAAAD DUDE TACKLE OUR FINAL CHALLENGE?
YEAAAHHH!!!
AND YOU KNOW WHAT'S ON THE LINE HERE, REX...
A TON OF RAD PRIZES INCLUDING A LIFETIME SUPPLY OF PIZZA...
NOT TO MENTION, ETERNAL GLORY AWAITS YOU ON...

PIZZA MOUNTAIN!
MEH.
Pizza Mountain®

I CANNOT BE THE ONLY ONE WHO THINKS SOMETHING'S UP HERE...
HMM?
YEAAAHHH! SQORK!
I MEAN, REX DIDN'T EVEN AUDITION TO BE ON THIS SHOW.
FREE PIZZA! COME TO PIZZA MOUNTAIN! SERIOUSLY, NOT A TRAP.
ALL WE GOT WAS THIS WEIRD LETTER. SEEMS A BIT HOKEY, AND FRANKLY, LIKE A TRAP.
WHAT'S THAT, LESLIE? I WASN'T PAYING ATTENTION.
NOT DUE TO BOREDOM, THOUGH. I JUST DON'T CARE ABOUT ANYTHING ANYMORE.
HEY! AREN'T YOU THAT SCIENTIST WHO CONTINUES TO EMBARRASS HIMSELF?
WH--?
NO!
LOCAL SCIENTIST
CONTINUES TO EMBARRASS SELF
SCIENCE TIMES

I MEAN, THE HOST IS EVEN ACTING STRANGE...
IT'S ALL A BIT OFF, Y'KNOW?
WH--?! WHAT ARE YOU DOING?
WHAT'S THAT?
RELAX. IT'S JUST SOME SUPER BUBBLES I CONCOCTED IN THE LAB.
SQORK WANTS SOME! LEMME SEE!
FIRST OFF, YOU SEE WITH YOUR EYES, NOT YOUR HANDS.
AND SECOND...
NO! I'M THIRSTY!
AHEM, I'M SQORK... NICE TO MEET YOU, THIRSTY.
GET IT?! CLASSIC!
UGH. I HATE EVERYTHING.
ALSO, THE HOST'S FACE LOOKS FUNKY... LIKE A MASK OR SOMETHING, RIGHT?

THIS IS NEVER GONNA WORK.
WELL, WITH THAT ATTITUDE, IT WON'T.
ON AIR
HEY! KEEP IT DOWN! THIS THING ISN'T GONNA DIRECT ITSELF!
LITTLE TOO INTO IT...
SORRY, I JUST DON'T SEE HOW WE'RE SUPPOSED TO TRAP THAT DINOSAUR AT THE TOP OF THAT MOUNTAIN. HE'S TOO RAD.
LOOK, IN THESE SITUATIONS I FIND THAT JUST FOLLOWING ORDERS AND DOING MY BEST IS ALL I CAN DO.
SIGH. I WILL DO MY BEST.
THAT'S ALL YOU CAN EVER DO, MAN.
urggghhh...
AND WHAT'S WITH THIS DUDE AGAIN? CAN WE TAKE THAT DUMB BAG OFF HIS HEAD? HE'S PROBABLY SUFFOCATING.
NO! WE WERE GIVEN DIRECT ORDERS THAT UNDER NO CIRCUMSTANCES WERE WE TO TAKE THAT BAG OFF!

NO! DON'T!
JUST BY TELLING ME NOT TO, YOU ARE FIGURATIVELY BEGGING ME TO DO THE OPPOSITE.
GASP!
N AIR
ugggHhh... heeeeellllp meeeeee...
I'M GONNA HURL.
WELP, THIS HAS TAKEN A DARK TURN.
LIKE I SAID, NOT ONLY DO YOU GET A LIFETIME SUPPLY OF PIZZA, BUT ALSO THESE FABULOUS PRIZES...
...A PALLET OF BLOWTARTS BRAND TAFFY POPS...
...A SEASON PASS TO SICK FLAGS THEME PARK...
...AND THIS ONE-OF-A-KIND KOWABUNGA KEY-TAR!
BLOWTARTS

GAAASSSPPP!
HOLY MOLY, I THINK YOU JUST SUCKED ALL THE OXYGEN OUTTA THIS ROOM.
SHUT UP! I WANT THAT KEY-TAR! I NEED IT!
JEEZ, OKAY! MAYBE YOU SHOULD BE DRINKING MY SODA.
GASP!
SQORK WANTS THOSE BLOW-TARTS!
EVERYONE STOP GASPING!
YOU STARTED IT.
WHEN?!
CHAPTER ONE, PANEL 1, DUH.
UGH!
EVERYONE HUSH UP! THEY'RE BACK FROM COMMERCIAL!
BACK AGAIN WITH OUR CHAMPION PREPARING HIMSELF FOR OUR FINAL CHALLENGE!

THIS IS IT, MY MINIONS...
ALL I ASK OF YOU IS YOUR COURAGE...
...AND YOUR WILLINGNESS TO DIE FOR OUR NOBLE CAUSE.
OH! THAT'S ALL SHE **NEEDS?!**
SHUT UP, MAN! YOU WANNA GET US KILLED?!
WHAT'S THE DIFFERENCE IF IT'S HER OR THE DINOSAUR?
VALID POINT.
AND WHY ARE WE EVEN PUTTING ON SAFETY GEAR?
LIKE A HELMET IS GONNA--
WHAT'S THE SAYING? NO **GUTS**, NO GLORY?
THERE WERE A MILLION OTHER WAYS TO MAKE THAT POINT.

AAAAND HE'S OFF!
DUDES AND DUDETTES, REX RADITUDE IS ENTERING PIZZA MOUNTAIN!
IT LOOKS LIKE REX HAS COMPANY ON THE HALF-PIPE FROM HECK!
AND NOW, LIGHT AS A FEATHER, HE HOPS OVER THE CHEESY-LAVA SLO-FLO!
I DON'T BELIEVE IT! REX IS ACTUALLY GRINDING UP THE RAIL OF NO RETURN!

HE MAKES LIGHT WORK OF OUR **LAZY RIVER...** HIS ENEMIES UNABLE TO HANDLE EXPOSURE TO **SHEER LAZINESS!**
HE'S EVEN MADE IT THROUGH THE **HOLE-IN-ONE!** GRANTED, IT WAS PIZZASAURUS-SHAPED. WHATEVER.
HOLY SMOKES! REX SIMPLY BUSTS THROUGH **SLIME-Y FALLS!** HOW DOES HE DO IT?!
NO. FREAKING. WAY.
HE'S DONE IT! LADIES AND GENTLEDUDES, OUR NEW GRAND CHAMP, REX RADITUDE!
RIGHT WHERE I WANT YOU...
WIN

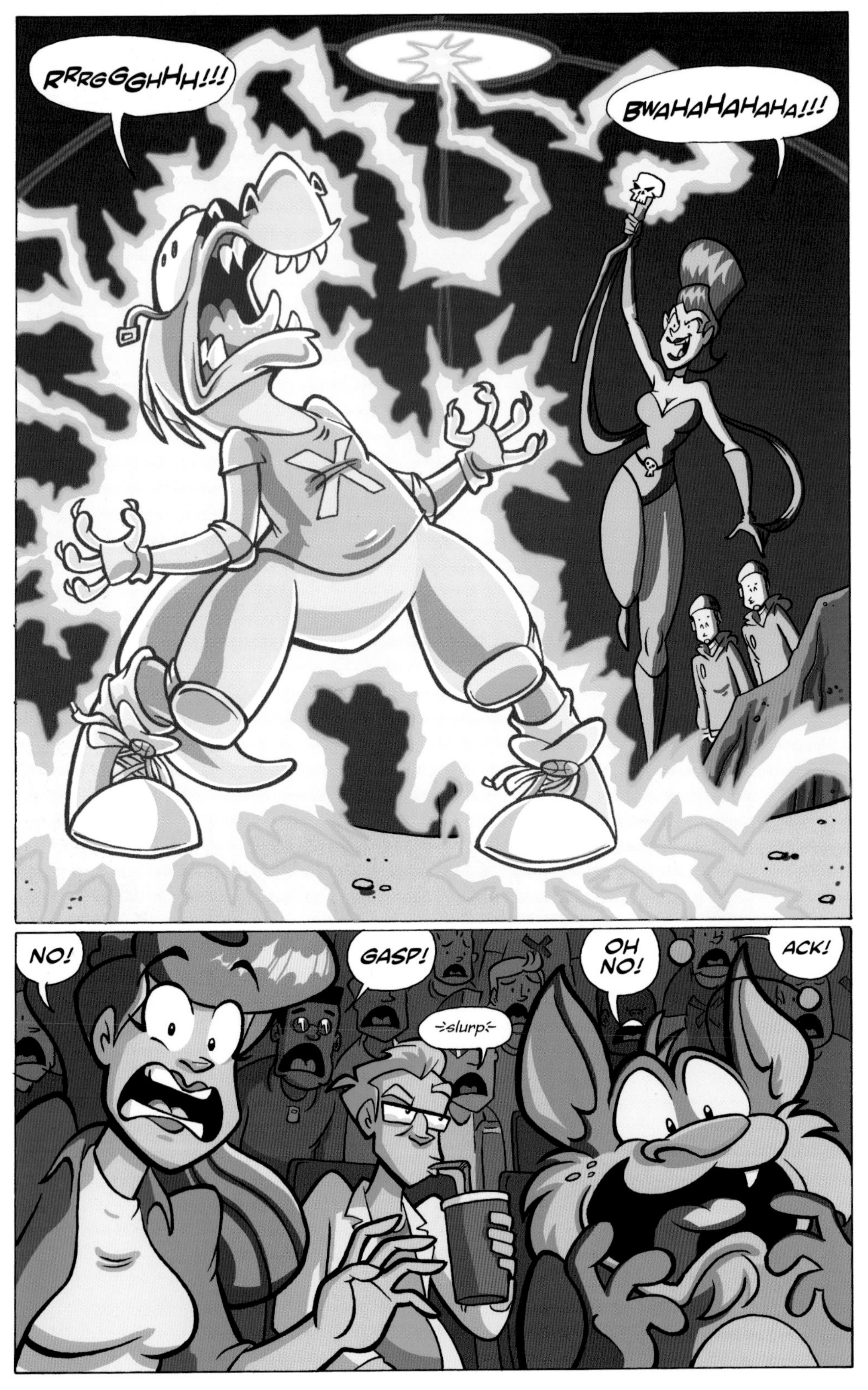
RRRGGGHHH!!!
BWAHAHAHAHA!!!
NO!
GASP!
~slurp~
OH NO!
ACK!

HOW CAN YOU SIT THERE AND SLURP THAT SODA?!
DON'T YOU CARE?!
-slurp- I WILL REFER YOU BACK TO PAGE 62, PANEL 3, IN WHICH I CLEARLY STATED THAT I DO NOT.
SQORK?!
OH, LIKE HE'S GONNA HELP. HE'S HAVING ONE OF HIS FULL-BLOWN FREAKOUTS.
WAITER! -hic- REFILL!
I'M NOT A WAITER!
STILL -hic- DOESN'T SOLVE MY PROBLEM!
SOMEONE...
---HAS TO...
---TAKE CONTROL!
MAN, THAT HOT CHICK'S GONE MENTAL!

JUST A FEW MOMENTS MORE AND YOU WILL BE DRAINED OF ALL RADICALITY!
WAY TO FALL FOR THE MOST OBVIOUS TRAP EVER, YOU DUMMY!
JEEZ, YOU ALREADY BEAT HIM... NAME-CALLING IS JUST RUDE.
SHH! WHAT'RE YOU, CRAZY?!
I'M SORRY, DID YOU CALL MY METHODS INTO QUES-TION?
I SURE DID.
SHUSH UP, DUDE!
NO! YOU SHUSH!
AND YOU SHOULD SHUSH TOO! IN FACT, I FEEL SORRY FOR YOU!
YOU'RE ALWAYS ANGRY BECAUSE YOU'RE SAD AND LONELY AND NOBODY LIKES YOU!
I-I-I'M...
Y'KNOW WHAT?!
I'M SORRY...

SORRY THAT I'M GONNA HAVE TO KICK ALL YOUR BUTTS.
WAIT...
WHY WOULD I BE SORRY?
CAN I START OVER?
WHAT'S THE OPPOSITE OF SORRY?
UNREPENTANT.
JUST LIKE THIS BEATDOWN YOU ARE ABOUT TO RECEIVE.
WHATEVER...
TRANSFORMATION SEQUENCE!

SQORK DOESN'T KNOW WHAT IN THE LISA FRANK IS GOING ON, BUT DOES KNOW THAT IT IS *AWESOME!*
LOOK! THE RADICALITY!
I *-hic-* HAVE EYES!
WHICH I WILL NOW CLOSE...
...TO TAKE A NAP...
...THAT I HOPEFULLY WILL NEVER WAKE UP FROM.

OUTRAGEOUS BEAM ENGAGED!
SUCK ON THAT!

NO...

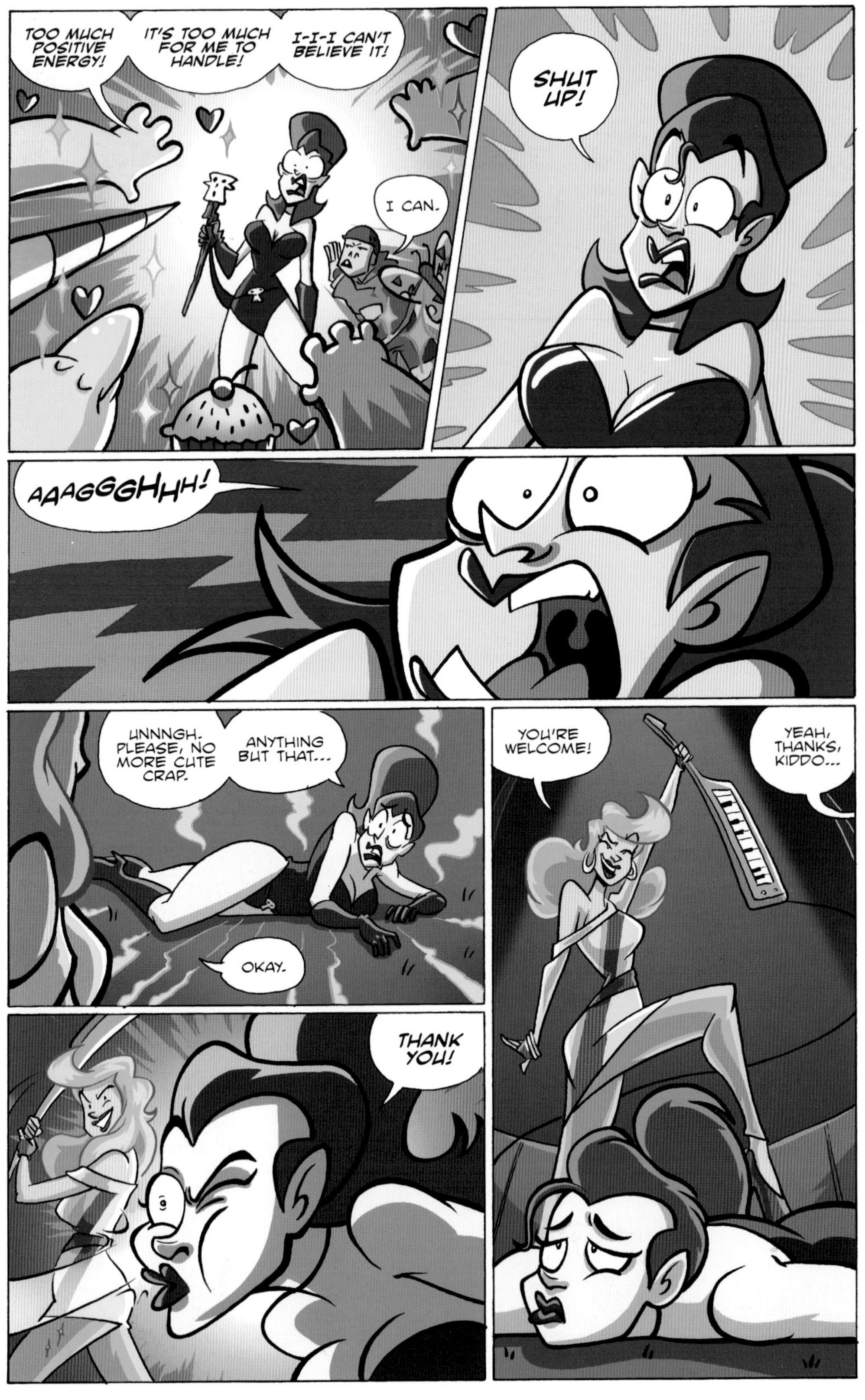

TOO MUCH POSITIVE ENERGY!
IT'S TOO MUCH FOR ME TO HANDLE!
I-I-I CAN'T BELIEVE IT!
I CAN.
SHUT UP!
AAAGGGHHH!
UNNNGH. PLEASE, NO MORE CUTE CRAP.
ANYTHING BUT THAT...
OKAY.
THANK YOU!
YOU'RE WELCOME!
YEAH, THANKS, KIDDO...

REX! ARE YOU ALRIGHT?!
I'M GOOD... FEELIN' A LITTLE DUMB FALLING FOR SUCH AN OBVIOUS TRAP, THOUGH.
GUESS IT GOES TO SHOW, EVEN THE RADDEST OF DUDES CAN BE A REAL DINGUS SOMETIMES...
AND THAT'S WHEN A TRUE FRIEND STEPS IN AND PROVES THEIR AWESOMENESS.
LET'S HEAR IT FOR THE BADDEST CHICK AROUND!
LEXI LUV!
WOOHOO!
YEAH!
SQORK KNOWS HER!
I THINK I HAVE TO BARF--
NOPE.
DEFINITELY HAVE TO BARF.

ONE LAST PIECE OF UNFINISHED BUSINESS...
HEY YOU!
GULP.
LIKE ALL DUDES, I ENJOY A GOOD PRANK.
BUT I CANNOT STAND FOR IMPOSTERY.
SIGH. I KNOW.
I WILL SAY THAT YOU DO A PRETTY GOOD IMPRESSION OF THAT HOST GUY.
WOW. THANKS! THAT MEANS A LOT COMING FROM YOU!
YOU KNOW I GOTTA DO THIS, THOUGH, RIGHT?
IT WOULD BE AN HONOR, SIR.
THANK YOU!
RRGH! I CAN'T BELIEVE IT!!!

HOW CAN YOU NOT BELIEVE WE WERE DEFEATED AGAIN?
YEAH. HAVE YOU NOT READ THE BOOK THUS FAR?
SILENCE!
I NEED TO FORMULATE A NEW PLAN!
THINK HE'S HAVING A STROKE?
AGAIN?
ONE CAN ONLY HAVE SO MANY...
SHUT IT.

YES. I HAVE IT.
IT'S BEEN THERE ALL ALONG...
...RIGHT BEFORE MY EYES.
THE TV?
WANT US TO CHUCK A TV AT THEM?
COOL IDEA...
NO! THE SCIENTIST!
THE ONE THEY CALL DUDERMAN.
HE IS THE KEY.
HE IS THE POINT OF WEAKNESS.
ONE WHO SUCKS SO MUCH MUST BE EASILY MANIPULATED... WE WILL PIT HIM AGAINST HIS FRIENDS...AND HE WILL BECOME MY GREATEST WEAPON.
AND THEN WE CHUCK A TV AT HIS HEAD?
SIGH.
Zo

CHAPTER 4

YEAH!
WOOOO!
OH YEAH!
YAY!
HMM? WHAT ELSE SHOULD WE TOAST TO?
SIGH.
FFCFFF!
FUNNY FUN CENTER FOR FAMILY FUN!
GEE, LEMME THINK. UMMM...
HOW ABOUT RADICALITY?! WHICH WE ALL HAVE!
PART ZONE!
REX
LEXI
SIGH.
SIGH!

SIGH AGAIN!
SIR, I'M GOING TO HAVE TO ASK YOU TO KEEP IT DOWN.
AND I'M GOING TO HAVE TO ASK YOU TO KEEP IT UP!
MEANING, REFILL MY SODA! CHOP CHOP!
SIGH.
DON'T YOU SIGH AT ME, MISTER!
I'M THE ONE WHO SIGHS AROUND HERE!
PARTY
ANYONE ELSE NOTICE JEREMY HAS BEEN A LITTLE OUT OF SORTS, LATELY?
GLUG!
NOW THAT YOU MENTION IT, IT'S BEEN KIND OF A STEEP DECLINE INTO MADNESS SINCE THAT LAST CHAPTER.
ALL HE NEEDS IS A DOSE OF FUN THAT ONLY WE CAN PRESCRIBE!
OR ANTI-DEPRESSANTS.
WHAT? SQORK CAN'T HAVE AN OPINION?

C'MON, WE'RE GONNA GET JEREMY OUT OF THIS FUNK, ONCE AND FOR ALL...
LET'S JUST EASE HIM INTO IT... DON'T FORCE HIM TO DO ANYTHING... REMIND HIM WHAT A GREAT FRIEND HE IS...
...WELL, WAS... AND...
NO!
COME ON! COME HAVE SOME FUN WITH US!
I AM HAVING FUN!
THIS IS HOW I HAVE FUN!
WITH MY ARMS FOLDED!
YOU LISTEN TO ME!
YOU'RE HAVING FUN WHETHER YOU LIKE IT OR NOT!

BUMPY BOATS
HAHA! THAT GUY ISN'T HAVING FUN!
STILL NO FUN!

GAMES
NO FUN!
C'MON, JEREMY, HOW COULD A VIDEO GAME POSSIBLY HURT YOU?
PIZZA
REX
THE GAME
INSERT
[COIN[S]]
HAHA! THIS GUY IS AFRAID!
OF FUN!

THAT'S MY GUY! GET IN THERE!
WHO DO YOU WANNA PLAY AS?
I WANNA BE ME...I GOT SOME SICK SPECIAL MOVES.
I CALL ME! I'VE GOT SO MANY SWEET OUTFITS!
SQORK WANTS TO BE SQORK BECAUSE IT MAKES SENSE!
SELECT YOUR DUDE!
REX
SQORK
RAD
SUCKY
RAD
RAD
SUCKY
SOME OF THE CHARACTERS START SUCKY...
YOU JUST GOTTA LEVEL THEM UP?
WHATEVER!
LET'S JUST PLAY THIS STUPID THING!

L
J
YO, JEREMY, BE A BRO AND HELP US OUT, HERE!
S
R
YEAH, YOU GOT A SPECIAL...
USE IT!
WHAT THE FART?!
THAT'S MY SPECIAL?
DON'T WORRY... HERE, I'LL COME RESCUE YOU.
COWER IN FEAR!
NO!
I'M TIRED OF THIS CRAP! I'M TIRED OF BEING A LOSER!
I'M TIRED OF BEING ME!
WAAAHHH!!!

REST ROOM
I'M CONCERNED ABOUT HIM...
CLAW
I DON'T KNOW WHO I AM ANYMORE...
OH, BUT I DO. I KNOW EXACTLY WHO YOU ARE...
WHUZZAT?!

YOU'RE VERY IMPORTANT WHERE I COME FROM, DR. DUDERMAN...
VERY IMPORTANT TO OUR CAUSE.
DID... DID YOU COME OUT OF THE TOILET?
WHAT?! NO! I'VE BEEN WAITING FOR YOU!
OH, SOOO YOU'VE BEEN WAITING IN A BATHROOM STALL FOR HOURS LIKE A CREEP?
UGH!
IT WAS LIKE AN HOUR AND A HALF, TOPS!
AND THAT'S BESIDE THE POINT!
I'M HERE TO OFFER YOU SOMETHING!
NO OFFENSE, BUT I TEND NOT TO TAKE OFFERS FROM CREEPY LURKERS WHO LURK AROUND TOILETS.
I WASN'T LURKING! I WAS WAITING! THERE'S A DIFFERENCE! SHUT UP!
AHEM... I'M A FRIEND. YOU CAN TRUST ME.

YOU LOOK IN THAT MIRROR AND SEE SOMEONE WHO IS POWERLESS...
SOMEONE ALONE...
SOMEONE WHO SUCKS...
I'M HERE TO TELL YOU TO EMBRACE THAT.
LET IT TAKE OVER YOU.
THIS IS WHO YOU ARE.
LONG AGO, IT WAS PROPHESIED THAT ONE WHO WAS TRULY RADICAL WOULD DESTROY THOSE WHO SUCK ONCE AND FOR ALL.
THIS "RAD ONE" CAME IN THE FORM OF YOUR NEW FRIEND...
...THE PIZZASAURUS.
YOU ARE NOT LIKE THEM. DR. DUDERMAN.
STOP TRYING TO BE.
JUST AS THERE IS A "RAD ONE," THERE MUST ALSO BE A "SUCKY ONE." WHERE DO YOU BELONG, YOU THINK?
I-I DON'T KNOW--
WHAT'S THAT?!
I'M AFRAID THE FINAL FIGHT HAS ALREADY BEGUN.
TIME TO DECIDE WHO YOU REALLY ARE.
BZUMMMM!
ZAP!
ZIP!

HEY! LET'S SNEAK UP BEHIND HIM!
REX! BEHIND YOU!
PROBABLY SHOULDN'T HAVE SCREAMED THAT!
YA THINK?!
THANKS!
NO PROBLEM!
SEE THAT? THAT'S WHY WE ALWAYS LOSE. WE NEED TO ACT LIKE A TEAM.
HOW DO TEAMS ACT? THEY TAKE A TIME OUT?
SO NOW WHAT?
I DUNNO... THINK UP A GAMEPLAN?
GOOD CALL ON THE TIME OUT!
SHUT UP.

SIGH. BEHEADING, THEIR MAIN WEAKNESS.
AND SPEAKING OF WEAK-NESSES...
...WHY DON'T YOU TELL YOUR OLD PALS THE IMPORTANT DECISION YOU JUST MADE IN THE BATHROOM?
I-- UH...
I HOPE THAT DECISION WAS WASHING YOUR HANDS THOROUGHLY.
JEREMY, WHAT'S GOING ON?
WHY ARE YOU HANGING OUT WITH SOME BAD GUY?
TELL THEM... TELL THEM WHAT SIDE YOU'VE CHOSEN...
TAKE YOUR RIGHTFUL PLACE BY MY SIDE...
DO IT.

NO! I CAN'T DO IT!
I ADMIT I'M A DORK, ISN'T THAT ENOUGH?!
LET ME COWER IN FEAR IN PEACE!
SHH, SHH... IT'S OKAY... NO BIG DEAL.
IT... IT'S NOT?
NOPE.
CUZ I CAN JUST EXTRACT WHAT I NEED FROM YOU!
SHRIEK!
THAT'S RIGHT! SHRIEK AWAY, DORK!
GASP!
LET HIM GO!

AFRAID I CAN'T DO THAT...
...THIS GUY HAS ALL THE RIGHT STUFF!
OH, SHUT UP, CREEP.
YOU SHUT UP!
BECAUSE I'M NOT A CREEP!
AND BECAUSE THIS IS MY BIG MOMENT!
THAT'S RIGHT, DUMMY DINOSAUR. I GOT AN INJECTION OF PURE, STICKY DORK JUICE FOR YA!
UGH... SUCH A CREEP.
SHUT UP!
CRUD!
GASP!

YES!
GASP! GASP AT THE POWER OF THE DORK SIDE!
POSERS! DESTROY THEM!
OR AT LEAST BUY ME SOME TIME!
REX!

LOOK OUT!
UNGHHH!!!
ugh...
NO.
GRRRR!
NO!

RAAAGGGHH!!
GULP.
ROAR!
CALM DOWN, BUDDY ...
PLEASE?!
GLUG!

I-I-I DON'T BELIEVE IT...
DID THAT JUST HAPPEN?
I CAN'T WRAP MY BRAIN AROUND THIS.
SHUT UP... YOU'RE RUINING THE MOMENT.
WHAT DO WE DO NOW?
WHAT ***DON'T*** WE DO NOW?!

WE HAUL THESE TWO BACK TO OUR DIMENSION...
HOPEFULLY, THE OTHERS HAVE FIXED DR. DUDERDUMMY'S *R.A.D.* PORTAL THINGY.
SPEAKING OF, WHAT DO YOU WANT TO DO WITH HIM?
MEH, WHO CARES? HE'S A WASTE OF SPACE ANYWAY.
AND WHILE YOU'RE AT IT, WHY DON'T WE TAKE SOME OF THESE VIDEO GAME CONSOLES?
Y'KNOW, SPRUCE UP THE OLD LAIR?
ANYTHING ELSE YOU WANNA STRAP TO OUR BACKS?
YAY! BAD GUYS WIN!
unnghhh...

WHAT HAPPENED? WHERE IS EVERYONE?
YOU TOOK A NAP. THE BAD GUY WON. NOW EVERYONE IS GONE.
I DIDN'T TAKE A NAP!
OH, SORRY, BY "NAP" SQORK MEANT "PASSED OUT FROM OVERWHELMING FEAR."
WHATEVER. DID THEY SAY WHERE THEY WERE GOING?
BAD GUY SAID SOMETHING ABOUT USING YOUR R.A.D. THINGY.
GASP!
WE'VE BEEN OUT AT MALLS AND GAME SHOWS AND FUN CENTERS THIS WHOLE TIME AND THE BAD GUYS HAVE BEEN WORKING ON MY R.A.D. MACHINE SO THEY COULD GET HOME!
I'M THE WORST.
ONLY IF BY "WORST" YOU MEAN "SO COMPLETELY DISCONNECTED FROM REALITY AND UTTERLY CRIPPLED BY FEAR, YOU LET YOUR FRIENDS BE CAPTURED BY BAD GUYS WHO ARE MOST LIKELY TORTURING THEM AS WE SPEAK."
THEN YES...
...THE WORST.

PIZZARELLAVERSE, BAD GUY LAIR, DUH...
WELL, I HOPE YOU ENJOY YOUR STAY IN OUR LAIR...
NOT!
HAHAHAHA!!
WELL, WE'VE DONE IT. THE FORCES OF RADICALITY ARE CONQUERED.
SOON, LIKE DOMINOES, ALL THINGS RAD ACROSS THE UNIVERSE WILL FALL!
AND IT'S ALL THANKS TO OUR OWN SERGEANT SURGE!
OH, REALLY? AND NO THANKS TO THE COUNTLESS POSERS WHO GAVE THEIR LIVES FOR THIS DUMB CAUSE!
DO YOU REALLY, ACTUALLY CARE?
NAH, NOT REALLY... JUST WANTED TO GET FIRED UP ABOUT SOMETHING.

AND THANKS TO THE COUNTLESS POSERS WHO GAVE THEIR LIVES FOR THIS GREAT CAUSE!
TAKE THE DAY OFF OR SOME-THING.
HOW DO YOU WANNA DISPATCH OF OUR NEW GUESTS?
WHY SO EAGER, SURGE?
LET US REVEL IN THEIR NEWLY ACQUIRED DORKINESS...
THEN, WE SHALL DESTROY THEM!
WH--WHAT HAPPENED?
I FEEL SO DRAINED...
REX?! ARE YOU--
SHHH!
CAN'T YOU SEE I'M TRYING TO ENJOY MY LATTE AND THIS NEW YORKER ARTICLE WHILE LISTENING TO PUBLIC RADIO?
NoOOOO!

NoOOOO!
CLOSED
WELL, LOOKS LIKE THEY BUSTED IT UP REAL GOOD...
NO GETTING TO THE OTHER DIMENSION ANY TIME SOON, I SUPPOSE.
RAD
RAD
SQORK DOESN'T THINK SO...
SEE? IT'S JUST UNPLUGGED.
NAH, I DON'T THINK IT WORKS ANYMORE.
OH MAN, THAT SUCKS, AMIRITE?
SEE?! IT WORKS!
RAD
I DON'T WANNA SEE...
...I'M AFRAID...
WHAT'S THAT? SQORK CAN'T HEAR YOU OVER THIS R.A.D. MACHINE CLEARLY WORKING AND WAITING FOR YOU TO GET INTO IT AND RESCUE OUR FRIENDS!
I'M AFRAID! OKAY!

AND I'M TIRED!
TIRED OF BEING SUCH A DORK!
SUCKING MY WHOLE LIFE!
AND I CAN'T DO ANYTHING TO CHANGE IT!
I HAVE NOTHING LEFT. NOT EVEN FRIENDS...
ASIDE FROM SOME KINDA TALKING PURPLE CAT THING...
NO OFFENSE.
NONE TAKEN.
WAIT... IF I REALLY HAVE NOTHING TO LOSE, WHY NOT TRY TO RESCUE THEM?
I MEAN, I KNOW I'M GONNA LOSE, BUT I COULD AT LEAST GIVE IT A SHOT!
EITHER I DIE HERE, ALONE... OR I DIE OVER THERE... TRYING.
SOOOO WIN-WIN, RIGHT?

CHAPTER 5

HAHAHA! YES!
OW!
WILL YOU STOP IT?!
HAHA! I COULD DO THIS ALL DAY!
OW!
HAHA! I COULD WATCH THIS ALL DAY!
OH, I'M AFRAID WE CAN'T DO THAT, SIR...
KICK ME
HE STILL NEEDS TO BE WEDGIED AND SWIRLIED...
...AND THOSE LOCKERS JUST CAME IN, SO WE CAN SHOVE HIM IN ONE.
IT'S GOING TO BE A BUSY DAY.
YOUR COMMITMENT TO BULLYING ASTOUNDS ME. GOOD WORK.
OH, THANKS. I'M JUST SUPER INTO MAKING LISTS.
AT FIRST IT WAS A WAY TO KEEP THINGS ORGANIZED, BUT NOW IT'S LIKE A SICKNESS WITH ME.
OR SOMETHING.
SOB.
OH, QUIT YOUR SOBBING, DRAMA QUEEN! YOU'RE RUINING THE BEST DAY OF MY LIFE!
JEREMY... WHERE ARE YOU?

OUCH!
REALLY?! POKING ME WITH A STICK?!
HUH HUH! YEAH!
I'M REALLY SORRY ABOUT THIS...
JUST FOLLOWING ORDERS, Y'KNOW?
HEY! LESS TALKING AND MORE POKING, YOU IDIOT!
YOU'RE ALL NOT VERY CREATIVE, ARE YOU?
AGAIN, APOLOGIES.
YOU SHUT UP AND ENJOY YOUR PUNISHMENT!
OR WAIT... DON'T ENJOY IT?
YEAH! DON'T YOU DARE ENJOY IT!
C'MON, JEREMY...
SERIOUSLY, THIS IS HURTING ME MORE THAN IT'S HURTING YOU.

THE TIME HAS COME...
THIS DUDE IS ABOUT TO MAN UP.
SQORK'S GLAD YOU FEEL THAT WAY, BUT IT'S NOT LIKE YOU HAVE A CHOICE.
YEAH, WELL, YOU COULD'VE GIVEN ME A COUPLE MINUTES TO PACK SOME STUFF BEFORE--
RAD
OOPS! SQORK PURPOSELY KICKED YOU!
AAAGGGHHHH!!!
RAD

WOWSERS!
AAAGGGH! I HATE YOU!

OOOF!
STOP THIS CRAZY THING!
OKAY, OKAY!
UNGH!
WOW, THANK GOODNESS FOR THAT SOLID BOULDER AND YOUR FACE WITH ITS AMAZING STOPPING ABILITIES, RIGHT?
SEE? YOU'RE NOT WORTHLESS!
GROAN.
WAIT, WHO SAID I WAS WORTHLESS?
OH, UH, NOBODY...
HEY! HOW ABOUT THAT TRIP, HUH?
LOOK, I'M TRYING MY BEST, HERE... TRYING TO BE WORTH-FUL FOR A--
HOLY CRUDMONKEYS.

CRUDMONKEYS, INDEED...
BUT WHERE THE HECK WOULD A BAD GUY LAIR BE AT?

SQORK IS GONNA GO OUT ON A LIMB AND SAY IT'S THE PLACE SHAPED LIKE THE BAD GUY'S HEAD.
AHEM, YES.
LOOK, JUST BE PATIENT WITH ME. I'M TAKING THIS WHOLE RESCUE MISSION MOMENT TO MOMENT.
GOOD IDEA. SQORK FINDS THAT WHEN HE LETS GO AND FOCUSES ON THE PRESENT MOMENT, GOOD THINGS COME TO HIM.
WOW, YOU'RE WISE.
OF COURSE, BAD THINGS COULD HAPPEN, BUT IT'S HOW YOU CHOOSE TO REACT THAT MAKES A DIFFERENCE.
JEEZ, YOU'RE LIKE A FORTUNE COOKIE... I FEEL LIKE A JERK FOR NEVER LISTENING TO YOU.
KIND OF LIKE HOW WE SHOULDN'T REACT TO THOSE BAD GUYS OVER THERE. THAT'S A BAD THING, BUT--
ACTION COP
RUN! RUN FOR YOUR FREAKING LIFE!
SIGH.

HEY, ISN'T THAT THAT ONE GUY?
COP
WHAT'S THAT?! I COULDN'T HEAR YOU OVER THE SOUND OF MY BACK BREAKING, CARRYING THIS DUMB THING ALL BY MYSELF!
ALSO, EH, WHO CARES? MASTER ALREADY HAS THE DINOSAUR AND THAT GIRL.
YEAH, BUT IF WE GET THOSE TWO HE'D HAVE THE WHOLE COLLECTION! HE'D PROBABLY SHOWER US WITH PRIZES!
LET'S DO IT!
SHOWERS!
PRIZES!
PANT!
PANT!
PANT!
WAIT UP! SQORK ISN'T THE BEST RUNNER!

YEAH, WELL, WHOSE FAULT IS THAT?!
WELL, SEEING HOW YOU CREATED SQORK... SQORK SAYS YOURS!
UMPH!
SQORK?!
HEH HEH, THAT'S MY NAME, DON'T WEAR IT OUT.
I'D SAY YOU'RE THE ONE WHO USUALLY WEARS IT OUT--OH, CRUD...
GO ON WITHOUT SQORK!
YOU'RE THE ONLY HOPE NOW!
SERIOUSLY, DON'T HESITATE TO--
RUN AWAYYYY!
SIGH.

AAAGGGH!
OH NO.
WHAT DO I DO NOW?!
I'M ALL ALONE!
I CAN'T THINK!
I JUST--
I NEED SOME--
SPACE!

WAAAGH!
ACK!
UNGH!
CRIPES...
CRIPES IS RIGHT...
OH, AND WE GOT YOU SURROUNDED.
SUCK ON THAT!

I BELIEVE IN HIM!
LOOK, I'M TELLING YOU, EVEN IF HE MADE IT HERE, HE'D BE TOTALLY WORTHLESS!
HAVE YOU NOT READ THE BOOK THUS FAR?!
I DON'T CARE WHAT YOU SAY...
YEAH, WELL, I DO CARE! I CARE THAT YOU'RE NOT TAKING YOUR PUNISHMENT SERIOUSLY AND THAT YOU'RE CLINGING TO HOPE!
KNOCK IT OFF!
HE'LL COME FOR US... YOU'LL SEE.
AND THEN WHAT?
NOTHING CAN STOP US NOW!
WELLLL...
WHAT?! WHAT IS IT?!
OH, NOTHING... IT'S JUST--
WHAT?! SAY IT!
THERE IS THAT ONE THING...
WHAT ONE THING?

PSST...
PSST...
...SECRET...
PSST...
...CHOSEN ONE...
PSST...
...SWORD OF POWER.
OH, RIGHT, FORGOT ABOUT THE PROPHECY...
BUT C'MON, LIKE THAT WOULD HAPPEN?
I MEAN, IT'S JUST ALLEGORICAL ANYWAY, RIGHT?
RIGHT?
SURE?
HONESTLY, I THOUGHT IT WAS MORE OF A METAPHOR.
FOR WHAT?

YOU'RE SURE YOU'RE NOT THINKING OF SIMILE?
ONOMATOPOEIA?
SHUT UP?
LOOK AT THIS STUFF...PIZZA FORESTS, PIZZA-CANOES. IT'S LIKE HE'S BEEN HERE.
BUT WHAT DOES IT MEAN?!
I'LL TELL YOU WHAT IT MEANS...
LOOK UPWARDS, DUMMIES!
FOR THE PROPHECY OF THE ***RAD ONE*** WAS WRITTEN IN THE STARS!
AND HE DOESN'T LOOK LIKE NO DINOSAUR TO ME...
LONG AGO, IT WAS SAID THAT ONE WHO EMBODIED ALL THINGS RADICAL WOULD RETURN TO HIS RIGHTFUL HOME.
FOREVER ALIGNING THE UNIVERSE TOWARD RADICALITY...
HE WOULD WIELD THE ***"KING SLICE"***...
A WEAPON FORGED FROM PURE RADICALITY, IT WOULD MAKE ITSELF AVAILABLE TO THE ***RAD ONE*** WHEN IT WAS MOST NEEDED...

THAT BEING SAID, NOTHING PERSONAL, BUT WE GOTTA BLAST YOU AND BE ON OUR WAY...
WE'RE MISSING A KILLER PARTY.
IS-- IS HE DEAD?
NAW. HE PASSED OUT IN FEAR AS SOON AS WE DREW OUR WEAPONS.
ONCE A LOSER, ALWAYS A LOSER.
SIGH.
HEY, MAN, SAVE THOSE SIGHS FOR WHEN YOU WAKE UP AT THE LAIR.
READY?
FINE.

SERIOUSLY?
WHAT THE--?
THESE THINGS SUCK!
TIME TO SHINE...

WHAT'S GOING ON?
I'M SCARED.
HOLD ME.
I HAVE THE POWER...
...THE POWER TO CALL UPON THE FORCES OF RADICALITY!
I AM JEREMY DUDERMAN, NO LONGER...

I AM DUDE-MAN!

GUESS IT WASN'T ALLEGORICAL AFTER ALL.
UH, DUH.
GAHHH!
RAAAGGGHHH!

TASTE THE CHEESY VENGEANCE THAT IS THE KING SLICE, BUTTMUNCHES!
NO--
JUST--
TOO--
RAD!

GASP!
WHAT? WHAT IS IT?
I JUST HAD ONE OF THOSE "THE-GUY-WHO-YOU-DIDN'T-THINK-WAS-GONNA-TAKE-HIS-RIGHTFUL-PLACE-AS-THE-RAD-ONE-JUST-HAS-AND-HE'S-COMING-TO-DESTROY-ALL-OF-US" FEELINGS.
YOU GUYS EVER HAVE THAT?
FINALLY.
I KNEW HE HAD IT IN HIM...
YOU GO, JEREMY DUDERMAN...

AH, THE SWEET SMELL OF PROLONGED JUSTICE...
SQORKETY SQORK! WHAT'S WITH YOU?
WHAT *ISN'T* WITH ME, IS THE QUESTION!
NOW, BASK IN PURE RADICALITY!
FOR TONIGHT, WE BANISH THOSE WHO *TRULY SUCK*, MY FRIEND!
SURE THING, BOSS!

RADICALITY AWAY!
IS THIS THE WAY YOU'RE GONNA TALK NOW?
I'M CONSIDERING IT...WHY?
EH, NOT DOING MUCH FOR ME.
HOWEVER, IT IS A LONG RIDE TO THE BAD GUY LAIR, SO YOU MAY WANNA THINK UP A CATCHPHRASE.
SUGGESTION MUCH APPRECIATED...
NOW, RIDE!

CHAPTER 6

HURRY! HURRY! C'MON!
GEEZ, WHAT'S THE RUSH?
I TOLD YOU! I HAVE THIS HORRIBLE FEELING SOMEONE'S COMING TO DESTROY US!
WE GOTTA GET RID OF THESE TWO AND GET THE HECK OUTTA HERE!
OH, WELL, AS LONG AS YOU HAVE A FEELING...
NO, HE'S RIGHT...
SOMETHING RADICAL THIS WAY COMES...
WHO ARE YOU?!
ME? I AM BUT THE INTERMEDIARY THROUGH WHICH FUTURE EVENTS ARE FORETOLD...
AND I GOTTA SAY, THIS NEXT BIT DOESN'T LOOK GOOD FOR ANY OF US!

WELL, THANKS!
WHERE WERE YOU, LIKE, FIVE CHAPTERS AGO?!
YOU'RE YELLING AT A BLIND DUDE... RELAX, MAN.
OKAY, IF YOU'RE NOT TOO BUSY, COULD YOU PLEASE DISPATCH OF OUR PRISONERS SO WE CAN AVOID THIS HORRIFIC PROPHECY?!
SEE? HOW HARD IS IT TO BE POLITE?
JUST DROP THEM INTO THE PIT ALREADY!
SIGH. SPECIFICALLY ASKED FOR "LOWERING."
UGH... HE'S REALLY TAKING HIS TIME, ISN'T HE?
WHAT'S THAT?
JEREMY?! THE GUY WHO LET YOU INTO OUR DIMENSION?
OUR ONLY HOPE?
HAHA! OH, BROTHER, DOES THIS CAT LOVE HIS LASAGNA!
SIGH.

RUMBLE!
WHAT'S GOING ON?!
IT HAS BEGUN!
THE TRUE RAD ONE HAS COME TO TAKE HIS RIGHTFUL PLACE AS RULER OF THIS DIMENSION!
REPENT!
BUT JUST TO BE SAFE, LET'S GET A FEW GUYS ON THAT DOOR.
SHUT UP!
UGH...JUST PUNCHED A BLIND DUDE...
ALREADY ON IT, BOSS!
IT'D HAVE TO TAKE SOME KIND OF RADICAL SWORD OF POWER TO GET THROUGH THIS!
JUST AS IT WAS FORETOLD!
SHUT UP.

CATCH PHRASE!
REALLY? THAT WHOLE JOURNEY AND THE BEST YOU COULD COME UP WITH WAS YELLING, "CATCH PHRASE"?
GASP!
I THINK IT'S KIND OF POETIC.

PREPARE TO SUCK SOME RIGHTEOUSNESS!
MEH, LITTLE BETTER...
WHOA, HEAD RUSH... GOTTA STAGGER THOSE GASPS FROM NOW ON.
CRUD.
RRAAAGHH!

RUN AWAY, FIRST TIER BAD GUYS!
SECOND TIER, ADVANCE!
WHAT'RE WE EVEN DOING ANYMORE?
I KNOW, MAN...I NEVER WANTED THIS FOR MY LIFE.
IT'S THE JOB, DUDE... YOU WORK SO HARD, SOON YOU BECOME THE JOB.
TRUE...BUT THIS IS WHAT WE WERE CREATED FOR.
SADLY, WE WERE BORN TO DIE.
I'M WEIRDLY FULFILLED!
SAME!

LEXI! REX!
HEADS UP!
OOF!
YOU-- YOU REMEMBERED MY NAME...
FINALLY, RIGHT?

IT'S OKAY...
NO, IT ISN'T.
I APOLOGIZE, LEXI.
I'VE BEEN A MAJOR LEAGUE BUTTHEAD.
AND YOU'VE ALWAYS BEEN THERE FOR ME.
EVEN WAY BACK WHEN, I WAS A TOTAL JERK, BUT YOU HELPED ME, STOOD BY MY SIDE...
AND DESPITE NOT CARING FOR ANYTHING BUT MYSELF, YOU BELIEVED IN ME...
YOU PROTECTED ME AND I DIDN'T DESERVE IT.
YOU ARE A TRUE FRIEND.

THAT BEING SAID...
RADICALITY RESTORED!
THANKS. I'LL BE GLAD TO PAY YOU BACK...
...BY KICKING SOME SERIOUS BAD GUY BUTT!
WELL, LOOK WHO'S BACK!
YOU'RE DARN SKIPPY I'M BACK.
AND I HAVE TO SAY...
...I'M PRETTY JEALOUS OF YOUR RADICAL LIFE TRANSFORMATION.
OH, "RAD ONE."
NOW WHAT SAY WE UNLEASH THE RADITUDE, HOMESLICES?

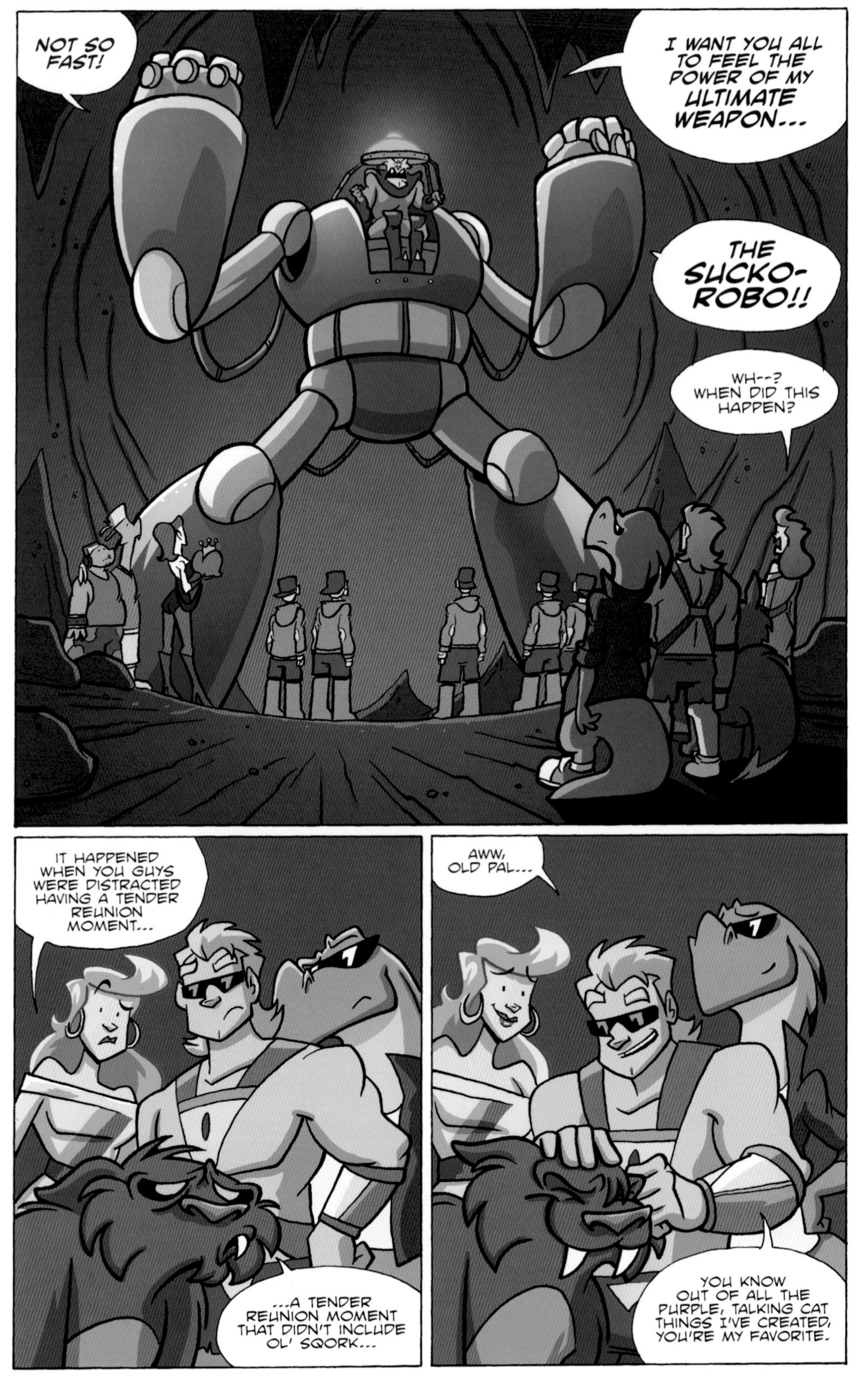
NOT SO FAST!
I WANT YOU ALL TO FEEL THE POWER OF MY ULTIMATE WEAPON...
THE SUCKO-ROBO!!
WH--? WHEN DID THIS HAPPEN?
IT HAPPENED WHEN YOU GUYS WERE DISTRACTED HAVING A TENDER REUNION MOMENT...
...A TENDER REUNION MOMENT THAT DIDN'T INCLUDE OL' SQORK...
AWW, OLD PAL...
YOU KNOW OUT OF ALL THE PURPLE, TALKING CAT THINGS I'VE CREATED, YOU'RE MY FAVORITE.

HEY!
AND SHUT UP!
SUCKO-ROBO BLOW!
NOT!

OH NO YOU DIDN'T...

OH YES WE DID!

ON SECOND THOUGHT...

YOU POSERS CAN HANDLE THIS...
...I BELIEVE IN YOU GUYS, FINALLY!
UGH.
RIGHT?
HEY!
WAIT!
SERIOUSLY!
HANG ON!
TIME!

LOOK, YOU GUYS ARE PROBABLY GONNA WIN THIS ONE...
SO IF YOU DON'T MIND, WE'RE GONNA TAKE OFF.
THAT COOL WITH YOU GUYS?
HMM, I DUNNO.
C'MON, MAN, YOU KNOW WE WERE NEVER REALLY INTO THIS.
DON'T YOU DARE ABANDON YOUR GLORIOUS LEADER!
I BROUGHT YOU INTO THIS WORLD AND I CAN TAKE YOU OUT!
AND SERIOUSLY, THAT GUY?
WE GET IT.
WHAT A DORK.
Y'KNOW WHAT? I FEEL FOR YOU GUYS...
TAKE OFF, FELLAS, YOU'VE EARNED IT.
THANKS, DUDES!
WAIT! WHY ARE THEIR HEADS NOT EXPLODING?!
LOOKS LIKE LIFE FOUND A WAY...
AS FOR YOU GUYS...

WEDGIES!
SWIRLIES!
NOOGIES!
RUGBURN!
AND YA BEEN PANTSED!

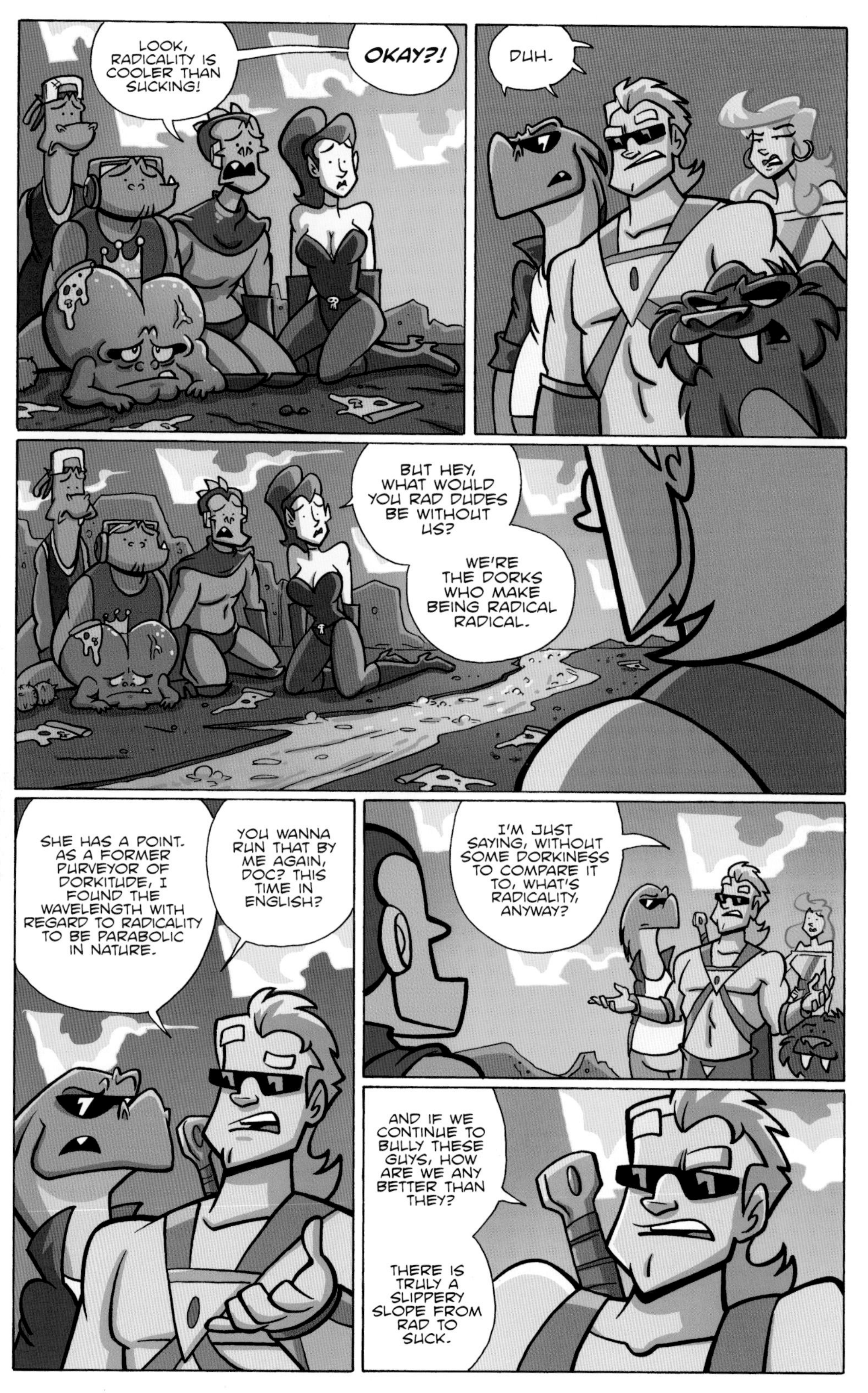

LOOK, RADICALITY IS COOLER THAN SUCKING!
OKAY?!
DUH.
BUT HEY, WHAT WOULD YOU RAD DUDES BE WITHOUT US?
WE'RE THE DORKS WHO MAKE BEING RADICAL RADICAL.
SHE HAS A POINT. AS A FORMER PURVEYOR OF DORKITUDE, I FOUND THE WAVELENGTH WITH REGARD TO RADICALITY TO BE PARABOLIC IN NATURE.
YOU WANNA RUN THAT BY ME AGAIN, DOC? THIS TIME IN ENGLISH?
I'M JUST SAYING, WITHOUT SOME DORKINESS TO COMPARE IT TO, WHAT'S RADICALITY, ANYWAY?
AND IF WE CONTINUE TO BULLY THESE GUYS, HOW ARE WE ANY BETTER THAN THEY?
THERE IS TRULY A SLIPPERY SLOPE FROM RAD TO SUCK.

I SAY THE TRULY RAD THING TO DO WOULD BE TO LET THEM GO.
LET THEM WANDER UNTIL THEY MAKE PEACE WITH THEMSELVES.
YOU CAN'T KICK US OUT INTO THE WILD!
THERE'S PIZZA OUT THERE!
SHH SHH, DON'T WORRY ABOUT IT...
THEY MAKE GLUTEN-FREE!
BUT IT TASTES LIKE GARBAGE!
OH, SHUT UP.
AND THAT'S THAT.

I'M TOTALLY PROUD OF YOU, DUDERMAN... WAIT, SORRY, DUDE-MAN.
I KNEW YOU HAD IT IN YOU.
I GOTTA ADMIT, THOUGH, I DID HAVE MY DOUBTS.
LIKE WHEN YOU COWERED UNDER THAT TABLE IN THE LAB...
...OR WHEN YOU COULDN'T EVEN DRIBBLE A BASKETBALL...
...OR WHEN YOU PASSED OUT IN FEAR AT THE--
YES!
WE GET IT ALREADY!
REGARDLESS, I THINK THIS THING WRAPPED UP PRETTY NICELY.
YEP. NO LOOSE ENDS TO SPEAK OF...
WELLLLL...

...I CAN THINK OF ONE...
CRIPES.
WAIT, WHAT THE FART? WE'RE BACK TO NORMAL?!
WHY AND/OR HOW?

RELAX... RADICALITY IS ALWAYS THERE WHEN YOU NEED IT. WITHIN YOU BOTH...
TRY AND ENJOY WHERE YOU'RE AT.
LOOK AROUND YOU!
YEAH, THIS PLACE IS A REAL **SLICE OF HEAVEN,** AMIRITE?
OH, SQORK! ***HAHAHAHA!***
WHAT'S REALLY FUNNY IS THAT WE HAVE NO WAY TO GET HOME!
HOLY COW, HE'S RIGHT.
I DUNNO... IS THAT SUCH A BAD THING?

IT KINDA FEELS LIKE WE ARE HOME.
Y'KNOW WHAT? YOU'RE RIGHT. I'VE NEVER FELT MORE IN THE RIGHT PLACE.
SO IT'S SETTLED.
WE'RE GONNA STICK AROUND.
ANYONE WANT SOME PIZZA?
DUH!!

THE END

Totally radical illustration by

BENJI WILLIAMS

(benjiwilliams.com)

PIZZASAURUS
REX

Wicked awesome illustration by

KEVIN MELLON

(kevinmellon.rocks)

JUSTIN WAGNER is a writer and illustrator (duh) living in Atlanta, Georgia. He's a storyboard artist and associate art director for FXX's *Archer*. He's drawn other books for Oni Press that you should totally check out, like *Rascal Raccoon's Raging Revenge* and *Do-Gooders*. He hopes you found this book to be most excellent.

Tubular illustration by Chi Sato (mochibabyart.com)

WARREN WUCINICH is an illustrator, colorist and part-time carny currently living in Durham, NC. When not making comics he can usually be found watching old *Twilight Zone* episodes and eating large amounts of pie.

Excellent illustration by Warren Wucinich

MELANIE UJIMORI is a Japanese letterer and vector artist from Hawai'i currently transplanted to Oregon. Bunnies will be the death of her one day, if the cats don't get her first. Visit her website at *www.merumori.com*.

Outrageous illustration by Melanie Ujimori

MORE GREAT COMICS FROM ONI PRESS

SPACE BATTLE LUNCHTIME, VOLUME 1: LIGHTS, CAMERA, SNACKTION!
By Natalie Riess
120 pages, softcover, color
ISBN 978-1-62010-313-5

SCI-FU
By Yehudi Mercado
144 pages, softcover, color
ISBN 978-1-62010-472-9

THE MIGHTY ZODIAC: STARFALL
By J. Torres, Corin Howell, and Maarta Laiho
152 pages, softcover, color
ISBN 978-1-62010-315-9

ALABASTER SHADOWS
By Matt Gardner and Rashad Doucet
192 pages, softcover, color
ISBN 978-1-62010-264-0

MERMIN, BOOK 1: OUT OF WATER
By Joey Weiser
152 pages, softcover, color
ISBN 978-1-62010-309-8

PRINCESS PRINCESS EVER AFTER
By Katie O'Neill
56 pages, hardcover, color
ISBN 978-1-62010-340-1

BAD MACHINERY, VOLUME 1: THE CASE OF THE TEAM SPIRIT
By John Allison
136 pages, softcover, color
ISBN 978-1-62010-387-6

ONI PRESS

For more information on these and other fine Oni Press comic books and graphic novels visit www.onipress.com. To find a comic specialty store in your area visit www.comicshops.us